The (Almost) Perfect
Guide to
Imperfect Boys

ALSO BY BARBARA DEE

Trauma Queen

This Is Me From Now On

Solving Zoe

Just Another Day in My Insanely Real Life

The (Almost) Perfect Guide to Imperfect Boys

Barbara Dee

Aladdin MIX

NEW YORK   LONDON   TORONTO   SYDNEY   NEW DELHI

ALADDIN M!X
Simon & Schuster Children's Publishing Division
1230 Avenue of the Americas, New York, NY 10020
First Aladdin M!X edition September 2014
Text copyright © 2014 by Barbara Dee
Cover illustration copyright © 2014 by Vera Brosgol
All rights reserved, including the right of reproduction
in whole or in part in any form.
ALADDIN is a trademark of Simon & Schuster, Inc.,
and related logo is a registered trademark of Simon & Schuster, Inc.
ALADDIN M!X and related logo are registered trademarks
of Simon & Schuster, Inc.
For information about special discounts for bulk purchases,
please contact Simon & Schuster Special Sales at 1-866-506-1949
or business@simonandschuster.com.
The Simon & Schuster Speakers Bureau can bring authors to your live event.
For more information or to book an event contact
the Simon & Schuster Speakers Bureau at 1-866-248-3049
or visit our website at www.simonspeakers.com.
Cover design by Karina Granda
Interior design by Hilary Zarycky
The text of this book was set in Plantin.
Manufactured in the United States of America 0814 OFF
2 4 6 8 10 9 7 5 3 1
Library of Congress Control Number 2014933151
ISBN 978-1-4814-0563-8 (pbk)
ISBN 978-1-4814-0564-5 (eBook)

For Alex, Josh, and Lizzy

ACKNOWLEDGMENTS

From-the-bottom-of-my-heart thanks to:

My agent, Jill Grinberg, for her wisdom and unwavering support;

My editor, Alyson Heller, for her expertise, enthusiasm, and openness;

Cheryl Pientka and Katelyn Detweiler, for nurturing this book from the beginning;

Bethany Buck, Fiona Simpson, Mara Anastas, Karina Granda, Katherine Devendorf, Vera Brosgol, Karen Sherman, Anna McKean, Carolyn Swerdloff, Emma Sector, and all the other lovely folks at Aladdin/ Simon & Schuster, for making publishing such a fun team sport;

Veronica Chang, Laura Burris Desmarais, Frances Kellner, Cheri Morreale, and Kym Vanderbilt, for being true friends to my whole family;

My mom, for always cheering me on;

Chris, for all of the above.

The (Almost) Perfect
Guide to
Imperfect Boys

CHAPTER 1

Today Wyeth Brockman became a Croaker.

Well, I mean, almost. Really close.

The way it happened was, he asked my best friend, Maya, if she'd seen this movie called *Battlescar III*. And when Maya said no (because seriously, why would she), Wyeth replied, "Well, I'm going this weekend."

His voice croaked on the word "weekend." Like it went "WEEK" (high pitch) "end" (lower pitch). And then he turned the color of a moldy strawberry.

For Wyeth, this was progress.

Okay, I'll explain.

A few months ago, Maya and I had divided all the

1

boys we knew into three categories: Tadpole, Croaker, and Frog. We'd even made a chart about it in my science binder: *The Amphibian Life Cycle (a.k.a. Finley & Maya's Super-Perfect Guide to Imperfect Boys)*.

First we named all the Tadpoles, the squeaky, silly little babies who belonged back in elementary school. Maya and I ignored the Tadpoles as much as possible. But it wasn't easy, because they were incredibly loud and obnoxious, the kind of boys who made fart jokes on the school bus.

Next were the Croakers, the boys who were starting to mature. Have you ever seen an actual tadpole turn into an actual frog? They go through this weird mutant in-between stage when they have fishy tails, but also reptile arms and legs. Croakers had croaky-sounding voices (hence the name), but that wasn't the grossest thing about them: They smelled like wet socks, or else like too much deodorant; they chewed with their mouths open; they stepped on your feet. But at least they talked to girls. Or rather, tried to talk to girls. Most of the boys we knew were Croakers; even in the eighth grade, they were definitely the majority.

Frogs were the highest form of middle school boy. What made a boy a Frog wasn't just that his voice had mostly stopped croaking; it was other stuff, like making eye contact with you in the hallway. Frogs were the boys who shared their homework, who laughed at your jokes, who'd discovered napkins. They weren't perfect, but they used shampoo. You could have a conversation with Frogs; they were the boys you could crush on. I'm not saying you *did*; I'm saying you *could*. But Frogs were rare in the eighth grade, and anyhow, the best ones were usually taken.

Up until today, Wyeth Brockman had been stuck at the Tadpole stage. In fact, considering the squeaky way he giggled, his obsession with LEGOs, the way he blew bubbles with his straw—plus the way he *never, ever* spoke to girls, even when they asked him a simple question—I thought he'd probably stay a Tadpole forever.

So when he asked Maya if she'd seen that stupid movie, this was definitely the first sign of Croaker behavior. It wasn't just the voice croaking and the blushing; it was the super awkwardness of the whole conversation. *I'm seeing a movie you would probably find excruciating. In case you wanted to know.*

Let me put it another way: If Wyeth had still been a Tadpole, he wouldn't have mentioned this stupid movie to a girl. He probably wouldn't have mentioned anything to any girl, period.

If he'd become a Frog, he would have added something like, *You're welcome to come to the stupid movie.* Or even, *Would you like to go to the stupid movie with me?*

But a Croaker couldn't make it to the invitation part. Maybe Wyeth didn't even realize he wanted to invite Maya. Maybe he just thought he'd share his moviegoing habits out loud, and if a girl such as Maya happened to be listening, well, all righty then.

A.k.a., totally Croaker.

All of this happened in social studies, where our teacher, Mr. Schiavone, had arranged the desks in "work stations" to "facilitate discussion." This month my "work station" consisted of me, Maya, Wyeth, and Jarret Lynch, who was the world's reigning Croaker champion, and also, by the way, not a nice person. No one (besides Maya and me) knew about the *Amphibian Life Cycle*, so I could have just announced Wyeth's upgrade to Croaker status. But if I had, Jarret would probably have gone, *Huh? What are you talking about?*

And the thing was, I didn't want to embarrass Wyeth. Or any boy, really; that wasn't the point of the *Life Cycle*, which was just about dealing with boy

4

immaturity. Which was a major issue, as any girl in middle school can tell you.

So instead I passed Maya a note: *CROAK???*

She smiled. Then she wrote back: *Hmm, mayyyybe...*

You didn't hear him croak just now? I wrote. *On the word "WEEKEND." Plus he kinda/sorta asked you out!!!*

Maya rolled her eyes. *No, he didn't, Finley. He just said he was seeing a dumb movie.*

Me: *That's a Croaker invite!*

Maya: *Please.* ☹

Me: *I'm putting it on the chart!*

She shrugged. And as soon as Mr. Schiavone started assigning the homework, I opened my science binder to the back. I glanced around to make sure no one was looking, especially Jarret. Then I flipped to the *Amphibian Life Cycle* chart, and next to Wyeth's name I wrote the word "Croaker."

Wyeth Brockman: Croaker.

But yeah, I had to admit it looked funny.

I thought about Maya's objection. We'd been doing the *Life Cycle* for about five months now, and whenever we upgraded any boy, we usually agreed on the change of status. So maybe she was right, maybe it was too soon for Wyeth—a single croak, a one-time blush, and a super-awkward invitation didn't qualify him for Croaker. *And besides,* I told myself, *just look at him:* He was chewing his thumbnail, which was a Tadpole thing to do, especially in public.

Still, Wyeth had made some actual progress today, and it would be wrong to ignore it. When a Tadpole evolved—even a fraction of an iota—it belonged on the chart, even if you couldn't figure exactly how.

So I erased "Croaker." I considered the options. Finally, this is what I wrote:

<u>Wyeth Brockman</u>: Tadpole with Croaker tendencies.

I liked this description; it seemed fair to me, and I felt sure Maya would agree with it eventually.

But even so, I wrote it in pencil, in case I needed to change my mind.

CHAPTER 2

At lunch I zoomed in on Maya's face. "Don't smile," I told her.

"Why not?" she asked through her teeth.

"Because it's so fake. You look like you're being photographed."

"I *am* being photographed."

"Well, okay, but you want to look normal, don't you? I thought that was the whole point."

"It is," she agreed, still doing this horrible *say cheese* sort of grin. "But don't normal people smile?"

"Sure. When there's a reason." I took a giant step backward, to get out of the streaky sunlight. Now a mysterious red icon was blinking at me, looking sort of like a spider waving a flag. I had no idea what my camera was telling me (yay for National Spider Day?), and I'd left the manual back in my bedroom. Dang.

I pressed a button, and the spider disappeared.

"Anyway, why should you be so ecstatic?" I asked Maya. "I'm just taking your yearbook picture."

"I'm ecstatic *because* you're taking my yearbook picture. So I don't have to use the zitty one."

"The other one wasn't zitty," I protested.

"Please, Finley."

"No, really, Maya. I thought it was nice."

But that was a lie, and we both knew it. Because for some nightmarish reason, on the morning of school photos, the Zit Gods had decided to zap Maya with a giant red dot on the tip of her nose. As soon as the photographer packed up his equipment and left, the Zit Gods took back their evil nose zit. But the picture was obviously forever, and even if the zit got photoshopped out, Maya's expression was: *Omigod, is that thing still there?*

Trust me, there was no way she could let that photo into the yearbook. Especially not in eighth grade, the year we were graduating from middle school, the first time yearbooks would even mean anything.

After the nose-zit incident, I'd offered to take a new shot of Maya with the digital camera my parents had just given me for Christmas. Maya and I had both agreed the photo should be candid, not pose-y. Except now she kept doing this generic fake photo smile, which in my opinion was worse than the nose zit.

"Fin? Can you please hurry?" Maya was begging. "It's freezing out here, and I think I'm going to sneeze."

"So sneeze."

"Yeah, right. That would make a gorgeous yearbook photo, don't you think? Snot spraying out of my nose . . ."

I zoomed out. No, too far. I zoomed back in. Better. "Listen, Maya, just do whatever you *feel* like doing. Don't worry about looking gorgeous."

"But I *want* to look gorgeous. If I wanted to look hideous, I'd just use the zit photo."

"It wasn't a zit photo." Mysterious Red Icon suddenly vanished. *Good. I think.* "Anyway, don't you want your photo to look a little bit different?"

"*Different?* You mean *weird?*"

"I mean unboring. Uncloney. Capturing your essence."

She raised one eyebrow at me.

"Okay, fine," I said. "No essence. What about an action shot?"

"Seriously?"

"Yeah, it could be cool. You could do a cartwheel." Maya was an amazing gymnast. She was only four foot eleven, but incredibly strong and agile. Next to my best friend, I looked like one of those Styrofoam pool noodles.

She ungritted her teeth. Suddenly she sprang into a cartwheel, ending in a bank of snow.

Click.

"How's that?" she asked, her shiny ponytail swishing.

"Great," I promised. "Perfect."

"Let *me* see." She grabbed the camera and squinted at the screen. "How do I find it? Oh. Well, it's *kind* of all right, but people won't see my face."

"Why do they need to? It's you being gymnastic." I took the camera. "And by 'people' we're talking about Dylan, right?"

"Puh-lease," she said. "I'm so over Dylan." She scooped up some snow and packed it into a ball. "Actually, didn't I tell you my New Year's resolution? I'm giving up on middle school boys."

"You are?" I said, laughing. "You mean including Wyeth Brockman?"

She didn't even bother to smile at that. "I mean all of them—Tadpoles, Croakers. Even the Frogs."

"Really? What's wrong with the Frogs?"

"Nothing," she answered. "Except they go to middle school."

I watched her throw the snowball. It landed way off, in the field between Fulton Middle School and Fulton High School, where the older kids hung out during the school day, cutting class or listening to their iPods or whatever they did when their teachers weren't looking. I knew Maya couldn't wait until next fall, when we would both be on that field, but to me it seemed the same as here, only bigger. Scarier.

The warning bell rang, meaning lunch was ending and Spanish was next on our schedule.

I blew on my fingers. "We should go," I said.

"No, wait, Fin, we still have four minutes." Maya was squinting down the field; she hated wearing her glasses, even though she was semiblind without them. "Hey, can you see who's that kid in the hoodie?"

I shaded my eyes from the low sun. I couldn't make out very much either, just a tall kid with dark hair standing over by the soccer net. Maya and I could name just about all of the ninth graders, and a few of the tenth, but this one didn't look familiar.

"Maybe he's a junior," I guessed.

"He couldn't be. If he was in my brother's class, I'd have seen him before this." She grabbed the camera. "Okay if I use the thingy?"

"You mean the zoom lens? Be careful."

"I won't break it; I'll just spy with it. What do I do?"

I showed her how to zoom in. "Just don't let him see you, all right?"

"Don't worry; I'm invisible. One of my many superpowers." She looked into the viewfinder. "Whoa. He's cute. I mean *really* cute. At least from here."

She took a few quick steps toward him, keeping the camera up to her face. "Although maybe we need a better angle."

"Are you serious?" I trotted behind her, my feet cracking the top layer of snow. "Stop doing that—he'll see you!"

"He's not even looking this way. Huh. Yes, definitely cute. No, definitely don't know him." She handed me the camera. "Want a peek?"

"This is so tacky." But I looked through the zoom lens at the boy, who'd started wandering around the net. His head was down, so I couldn't make out his face.

Suddenly he stopped walking. And looked up. Right at me.

"Oh, shoot, let's go," I muttered, yanking Maya's arm.

"Why?"

"Because he just saw me!"

"And?"

"*And* I was basically stalking him. This is a teeny bit awkward, don't you think?"

"It doesn't have to be. We could introduce ourselves."

"*You* could introduce *yourself*. Because he didn't see *you* following him around with a *camera*." I glanced over my shoulder. Now he was heading toward us, waving his arm, walking even faster than we were. *Oh, great, great, great.*

"Why is he coming this way if he goes to the high school?" I whispered.

"Maybe he dropped out."

"Don't joke, Maya, okay?"

"Maybe he's chasing us. Maybe he thinks we're paparazzi."

"Argh, this is excruciating."

Maya sighed. "All right, Finley, then just tell him the truth."

"The *what*?"

"Tell him I made you spy on him. Tell him—"

"Finley?" the tall boy called. He had a deep voice, not at all croaky.

I glanced at Maya in panic. Then I turned around.

The boy was a few yards away now, close enough for me to see that he had longish brown hair, high cheekbones, a narrow nose that pointed sideways at the tip, and blue eyes so dark they could qualify as purple. He was dressed in slouchy jeans, with a long black thermal and a light gray hoodie. Standard boy wear, nothing fascinating, so I took a second peek at his almost-purple eyes.

"Finley?" he repeated. "Finley Davis?"

"Yes?" I squeaked.

He grinned. "It *was* you. You had that camera covering your face, so I wasn't sure."

"No, yes, it's really me." I slipped the camera into my jeans pocket, so now it was bulging out of my thigh.

Lovely. "Um, I don't mean to be rude or anything, but do I know you?"

"Well, you did." He was watching my face. "But maybe you've forgotten. Zachary Mattison?"

I blinked.

No, I told myself. *It couldn't be.*

Because the last time I'd seen Zachary Mattison, he'd been a Tadpole. Actually, no—even less mature than a Tadpole, more like a Tadpole egg. A skinny, doofy little egg with a chirpy voice, sticking-out ears, and an incredibly obnoxious sense of humor.

And that was when? Not even a year ago? It was like he'd fast-forwarded through the whole *Amphibian Life Cycle*.

My mouth froze; I couldn't speak.

But Maya could. "Wait!" she shouted. *"Freakazoid?"*

"Yeah, exactly," the boy replied. "Freakazoid."

His smile changed, but he was still smiling.

CHAPTER 3

"Sorry," Maya blurted. "It just came out. I didn't mean—"

Zachary shrugged. "Hey, no problem. I've been expecting all that Freakazoid stuff. And I'm fine with it, in fact."

Maya shot me a look. "You *are*?"

"Yeah. I think it's funny." He blinked at me. "Don't you think it's funny, Finley?"

"Not really," I said, trying to spot his ears underneath the new hair.

The second bell rang, but we didn't move.

"So anyway. What are you doing here?" Maya asked, probably a little too curiously.

"Waiting for my mom," he said. "She's in with Fisher-Greenglass."

Maya and I exchanged glances. Ms. Sara Fisher-Greenglass was the principal of Fulton Middle. You were "in" with her only if you were "in" big trouble. Or possibly getting out of it.

"Huh," Maya said. "So that means you're coming back?"

"Maybe. Don't know yet."

"Then you might? Didn't you get expelled for fighting with Jarret?"

He looked surprised. "They said that? Oh no. Not expelled."

"So what happened to you, exactly?" She folded her arms across her chest, the way she did when she thought someone was lying. "You basically disappeared in the middle of seventh grade."

"It's kind of complicated," he said flatly. "You know, family stuff."

"Really? Like what?"

"Maya, we're late," I muttered. "Señor Hansen's going to kill us."

Zachary looked at me. "Hansen?" he repeated. "You have Hairy Hands for eighth-grade Spanish?"

"Yeah, we do," I said. "Unfortunately."

"How did *that* happen?"

"Who knows. Maybe he liked torturing us so much in seventh grade he wanted a second crack."

"But that's not fair," he argued. And right then he sounded exactly like the old Zachary, the one I remembered.

"Okay, well, we'd better get going, then," Maya said. "See you around, Zachary."

"Yeah," I said. "See you."

"Bye, Finley," he said, catching my eye.

Maya and I started running down the hallway. My legs were twice as long as hers, but she was still half a step ahead of me. "*Bye, Finley,*" she repeated. "What was I, invisible?"

"No, of course not. But you were sort of rude."

"How was I rude?"

"You called him Freakazoid," I said.

"*Everyone* called him Freakazoid."

"And you were grilling him about getting expelled. Like you didn't believe him."

By then we were almost outside Spanish, so we slowed down. "Well, sure," she murmured. "Don't *you* think it's slightly incredible that he's back, all of a sudden? In the middle of eighth grade?"

"We don't know what happened with his family," I pointed out. "And anyhow, he might not *be* back. He said *maybe*."

"Fisher-Greenglass wouldn't be meeting his mom just for girl talk, Fin."

"I guess."

I didn't say anything for a bit. Then I blurted out, "He did seem different to you, didn't he?"

"You mean Froggier?"

I laughed. "Well, yeah."

"What a shocker, right? Zachary the Frog. It was like he did all his Croaking in private."

"I know. Or maybe he jumped over the whole Croaker stage."

"He couldn't have," Maya insisted. "Croaker is when Tadpoles get legs. You can't jump if you don't go through the getting-legs stage."

"True." I glanced over my shoulder, but the hallway was empty. "Or maybe," I said, "he was just a totally different person."

By then we'd reached room 302, so we stopped.

"What do you mean?" Maya said, laughing. "Are you saying that cute boy was an *imposter*?"

"Well, it's possible, isn't it? He could be this normal,

cute Frog boy only pretending to be Zachary Mattison."

Maya covered her mouth. "Interesting theory, Nancy Drew. Except for one thing: why would anyone pretend to be Freakazoid?"

She turned the doorknob. As the door screeched open, it was obvious that the class was in quiz mode. Olivia Moss looked up at us in desperation, Chloe DeGenidis grumbled, and Jarret Lynch, well, grunted. I hated to even say that word to myself, "grunted," because it was such typical Croaker behavior. But he really did grunt, and so loudly that Kyle Parker punched him in the arm.

"Hola," Señor Hansen boomed from the back of the room. "You girls are now seven minutes late for my class, which I find extremely disrespectful. But instead of reporting you both to the principal, I'll allow you to wrestle with a little pop exercise."

"Fabutastic," Maya murmured.

Señor Hansen flashed a fiendish smile. This gave him a unibrow, one dark werewolfish fringe above his eyes. "Excuse me, Señorita Lopez, *what* did you say?"

"I said sorry we're late, Mr. Hansen," Maya answered calmly. She always called him that, "Mister" instead of "Señor"; if he noticed, he never said anything.

He hulked over and with his scary-hairy fingers gave us each a double-sided paper titled *Quiz #15— Irregular Verbs in the Preterit.*

Help, I thought.

I hadn't studied for this quiz, and even if I had, this was exactly the sort of thing I was horrible at. For me to memorize something it needed to make sense—I couldn't just mindlessly recite a list of meaningless verb variations. Whenever I was stuck studying history or science, Mom suggested memory tricks ("mnemonic devices," she called them)—silly rhymes and acronyms, mostly, but they made the facts stay in my head like friendly ad jingles. Except you couldn't use Mom's tricks for cramming irregular verbs in the preterit—you just had to drill them, over and over.

Plus the whole "preterit" business was ridiculously complicated. Why did the Spanish language need *two* past tenses—one for completed actions (the preterit) and another for past actions done over time (the imperfect)? It all seemed random and unfair, if you asked me.

I peeked at Maya, whose table was in the back of the classroom over by the windows. Totally apart from the fact that she spoke Spanish at home, my best friend was a superstudent, so of course she was already busy conjugating.

All right, Finley, get to work, I scolded myself. I took my chewed-up pencil out of the other pocket, the one without the camera. Somehow I made it through the first three conjugations, but by *numero quatro*, all I could think about was Zachary Mattison.

Not the one I'd just seen. I mean the Tadpole-egg version, the skinny, doofy little kid with the chirpy voice and the sticking-out ears, who wore rugby shirts in primary colors, and who was always telling the world's stupidest jokes. Jokes about boogers. Also about smelly armpits, fat butts, farts, burps, and other assorted body functions. Not to mention his specialty: jokes about people's names.

I remembered how crazed he made Chloe DeGenidis, insisting her name sounded like a disease. One time in the middle of the cafeteria, she yelled, "Zachary, I've *had* it, you are *such a total loser!*" Then she threw her cell at his head, and when it hit his forehead, he actually *laughed.*

Oh, and when he laughed, he usually fell on the floor, so a lot of the time he was dusty. Or smeary or full of crumbs. Which didn't do much for his Total Loser status, especially with the girls.

And of course neither did his obsession with gummies. Zachary had this thing for the grossest ones: worms, squid, octopi, slugs. (Did they even make gummy slugs? Whatever, you get the idea.) He'd chew them a little, get them soft and semiliquidy, then dangle them out of his mouth until people (specifically, female people) screamed, *"Eww, Zachary, stop!"*

Obnoxious, right?

And beyond-Tadpole immature.

One time he almost kissed me like that.

Well, okay, it wasn't intentional; he had leftover gummy spit on his face and he kind of bumped into me at the lockers. And when I turned my head to see who was stepping on my heel, Zachary's sticky lips were right there.

"Oh," he said. "Sorry."

"Wash your face," I snapped. "And watch where you're going!"

Which probably sounded like his mom or something, because he turned bright red.

"Zachary's kissing Finley," Jarret sang. "Zachary's kissing—"

"Your butt," Kyle announced, and everybody started laughing.

23

In seventh grade, our third year at Fulton Middle, Zachary finally stopped the dangling-gummy routine, but not the obnoxious jokes. Or the general social cluelessness. Chloe started having these huge-ormous parties in her basement (which is like half the size of the Fulton Middle School gym) and Zachary would just show up. Uninvited. People ignored him the first few times, but by the fourth party Chloe was furious. She waited until he was standing by the pizza; then she came over and said loudly, in front of like a dozen people, "Um, Zachary? Did someone ask you here? Because you know, *I didn't.*"

"But I did," Maya lied. Not because she felt sorry for him, she told me afterward, but because she hated how all of a sudden Chloe was acting like Miss Seventh Grade.

Except Zachary didn't even get that he was being saved. He didn't look at Maya, or thank her, he just took a huge gulp of Fanta, burped loudly, and commented, "Nice party for someone with *deginitis.*" Then he stood there guffawing like it was the most hilarious joke in the world.

So naturally everyone kept thinking: *Total Loser.*

Because let's face it, he was. I mean, even by seventh-grade Tadpole standards.

But the exact way he went from Total Loser to Freakazoid was something I never really knew, mainly because I'd stopped paying attention. That was because for some warped reason I still can't figure out, I was suddenly madly, hopelessly in crush with Kyle Parker. (It didn't even bother me that he was a Croaker with skin issues, or that he talked about nothing except boring football.) The crush was absolutely over by spring break last year, but it kept me from noticing other boys there for a while.

Anyway, my point is, for most of last year pretty much all that registered about Zachary was the Official Gossip. Namely, that he'd "freaked out" during some kind of fight with Jarret (as in, throwing things, throwing punches, generally "acting freaky"). During that fight, Jarret started calling him Freakazoid, and everyone else immediately followed. And according to the Official Gossip, Jarret's parents showed up at school the next day, demanding that Fisher-Greenglass kick Zachary out.

So she did.

At least, that's what everybody said.

After that no one saw him. Somebody's mom (I think maybe Kyle's) talked to Zachary's mom in the A&P and found out there were "family difficulties," which sounded like a polite way of saying "divorce." Somebody mean (I'm pretty sure Jarret) said that maybe when Zachary's parents split up, they flipped a coin to see who'd get stuck with Zachary. And Zachary's dad lost, so Zachary went off to live with him somewhere. Or maybe they'd shipped him off to Loser School, Chloe said. Like on another planet.

But whatever happened, here he was again now, back at Fulton Middle, as if he thought all would be forgiven. Or forgotten. Which, I'm sorry, was just insane.

I mean, if he wasn't crazy before, and he really thought he could just show up a few months before graduation, and everyone would be all, *Hey there, Zachary, long time no see,* he had to be crazy now. Because the thing about this school was, people remembered *everything*.

For example: Those dorky I ♥ Our Planet valentines I e-mailed to the whole class in fifth grade? Just a week ago Micayla Hoffman asked to borrow some loose-leaf paper, "or you could e-mail me some to heart our planet, ha ha."

Or the time in sixth grade when I trimmed my own bangs and ended up with a crooked fringe two inches above my eyebrows? Ben Santino *still* does this snipping-scissors motion when he passes me in the hall. I'm totally not exaggerating.

And if you compare those stupid things to what Zachary did, or anyway to the Official Gossip version of what he did—

"Time," Señor Hansen called. "Pencils down."

Olivia looked up. She was teeny, with beautiful cocoa-colored skin and almond-shaped eyes. Everything about her was adorable—she wore lots of pink, had a thing for Hello Kitty, and her voice chirped. "Oh, pleeeeease, Mr. Hansen, can't we have a little longer? The period's not even over yet."

"Tests are full period; quizzes aren't," he replied, as if he were reciting a rule from the Official Teacher's Handbook. "You just need to pace yourself better next time."

"I *did* pace myself. There were just too many conjugations!"

"Oh, come on, Señor Hansen," Chloe called out in this fake-sweet voice. "Why can't you give us five more minutes? We won't tell."

Jarret started laughing. Uncontrollably. In an embarrassing way that was almost Tadpole, actually.

Señor Hansen didn't answer. He snatched Chloe's

quiz, then Jarret's, and then hulked up and down the rows, snatching everybody else's. When he got to mine, he flipped it over to the mostly blank side.

"Was there a problem, Finley?" he asked, much too loudly for it to be private.

"Not really," I said. "I guess it's kind of a pacing thing."

"So if you *knew* time management was an issue, why were you late for class?"

"Um," I answered. Instead of: *Well, you see, we were kind of stalking Zachary Mattison. Who's a Frog but possibly also an imposter, because how else could he have skipped over Croaker? It doesn't make sense.*

Señor Hansen was staring at me. Waiting for my brain to click on.

Still waiting.

Still waiting.

"Mr. Hansen, it's all my fault," Maya announced. "I asked Finley to take my yearbook photo, and we lost track of the time."

"Finley's taking yearbook photos?" Olivia asked excitedly.

"Retakes," Maya answered. "Why? You want her to do yours?"

"Yes! Have you seen my picture? I look hideous."

"Olivia, dearest, you always look hideous," Chloe said. She yanked out her lobster-claw hair clip, shook her shiny, medium-brown hair, then gave herself a new messy bun/ponytail exactly like the one she'd just undone. What was bizarre was that everyone watched, like it was the coolest, most fascinating thing ever.

"Shut up," Olivia said, sticking out her tongue at Chloe. "I hate you, Chloe."

"Well, that's too bad, because I love you."

Maya flashed me a look like, *Excuse me while I barf.*

"Girls," Señor Hansen warned in a scary-quiet voice. "That. Is. Enough."

Olivia turned to me with begging hands. "*Would* you take my picture, Finley? Pleeease?"

"Sure," I said. "Although I just got the camera. And I'm not really—"

"She's amazing," Maya insisted. "Don't worry, it'll be great."

"*Excuse me,*" Señor Hansen bellowed. "But does anyone here realize they happen to be sitting in *my classroom*?"

"Sorry," Maya said quickly. She gave him her radiant smile, the one she usually saved for the end of her gymnastic routines. "I guess we thought, you know, Mr. Hansen, since there were only a few minutes left anyway—"

"That you could waste our precious class time discussing yearbook photos?" Señor Hansen dropped the quizzes on his desk with a thud. "You know what I think? I think maybe we should have a full-period *test* tomorrow. Because it seems *that's* the only way to get you people to focus on Spanish."

Everyone groaned.

Chloe did a fake-cheery smile. "Well, thanks a lot, Maya," she said sarcastically.

"It's not her fault," I murmured.

"Right, Finley, it never is."

I glanced at Maya, but she was pretending to copy the homework assignment. And turning a shade of red that was not fabutastic.

And I thought: *Zachary wanted to come back to this?*

I mean, seriously, you would have to be crazy.

CHAPTER 4

At dismissal, Olivia was sucking in her cheeks runway-style, which made her look like she was trying to whistle. Then she pushed her hair so that it fell over one eye. The other eye looked hurt. Like someone was stepping on her foot.

"Um," I said, as I looked up from the camera. "Actually, I think it's better if the photo is candid."

"You mean casual?" Her forehead puckered. "That could work. You have to do it soon, though. Because Sabrina says the yearbook deadline is Friday."

Sabrina Leftwich was yearbook editor. She was also starting center on the girls' basketball team. I was on the team too, but mostly I played bench.

"We can do it tomorrow," I promised Olivia. "But maybe you should just ask someone else."

"No, no. You *have* to take my picture, Finley. Please, I'm begging you."

We were standing on the steps in front of school, the way we sometimes did at dismissal. Don't ask why. It was one of those leftover rituals from when we were all best friends—Maya, me, Olivia, Hanna MacPherson. The four of us hadn't really hung out together since the days when we belonged to Green Girls, and played soccer every weekend, and spent Saturday nights in sleeping bags on each other's floors. It was weird—we'd never had a fight or anything dramatic like that, but we weren't a troop anymore, or a bunch of friends, either, really. It was mostly like every other day or so we four needed to check in with each other: *You still there? Cool. Okay, see you around sometime. Bye.*

Now Maya was walking over to us with Hanna, who sometime last year fell madly in love with her viola. On weekends she was in maybe three different orchestras, and on weekdays she was either taking lessons or practicing after school. It was a bit scary intense, if you asked me, but then, I'd personally never been all extracurricular.

"Omigosh," Hanna was groaning. "How do you guys *stand* it?"

"Hansen," Maya explained to Olivia and me. "I just told her about today."

"I am *so glad* I'm in the other Spanish class," Hanna exclaimed. "Señora Phillips made us guacamole. Then she taught us to rumba."

Olivia slapped the side of her head. "Are you serious? She's giving you guys food, while Hairy Hands is giving us—"

"Torture," I finished.

"*Pop exercises,*" Maya said. "Irregular-verb lists. Ack, Finley, can you believe I opened my big mouth?"

"You were incredibly brave," I said, patting her back.

"I was incredibly stupid. Now he's giving us a full-period test tomorrow, thanks to me," she informed Hanna.

"Sick sick sick," Hanna said. She flipped her long blond hair over one shoulder, and then stroked it, a kind of mermaid move. But she wasn't showing off her gorgeous hair; even though Hanna was pretty, she wasn't stuck-up about it. I mean, as far as I knew; I barely saw her these days, so I didn't feel comfortable having an opinion.

Maya caught my eye. "Speaking of sick."

I blinked. "What?"

"Didn't you tell O yet?"

"Tell me what?" Olivia's face lit up. She lived for gossip, I swear.

"It's not even something we know for sure," I said quickly.

"It's *probably* true," Maya corrected me. "I mean, obviously, right? Because of that meeting at lunch? With Fisher-Greenglass?"

"What meeting?" Olivia asked, fluttering her hands. "Pleeease tell us, you guys!"

Maya wound her purple wool scarf around her neck. Then she shifted her book bag from one shoulder to the other. She was waiting for me to say it, apparently. *Fine*, I thought. *I will.*

"Zachary Mattison is coming back," I announced.

"Who?" Hanna asked, glancing at her cell.

"Freakazoid," Maya said.

Olivia gaped. "Are you serious?"

"Uh-*huh*. Finley and I talked to him at lunch. He

still had to hear from Fisher-Greenglass, but—"

"And did he still have all those gummies hanging out of his—"

"No," I said. "He didn't."

"But wasn't he, like, kicked out of school for life?" Hanna asked.

"Apparently not." Maya shrugged. "Oh, and by the way, he's totally hot now. Ask Finley."

Hanna and Olivia looked at me.

"Yeah, I *guess* he's cute," I said, as if it had never occurred to me before right this second. "Cuter than he used to be. Taller. His hair covers up his ears and everything. But really, you guys, he's still Zachary."

"Although Finley is convinced he isn't," Maya said. "She thinks this new-improved version is an imposter."

"I was just joking, Maya, okay?"

"What do you mean, an imposter?" Olivia demanded. "You mean like those high school kids who got paid to take that test?" At Fulton High a bunch of kids were caught cheating on an SAT, so we'd been hearing about it nonstop from Fisher-Greenglass. Every Thursday this semester she'd been lecturing us in an assembly called Transitioning to High School, except all she ever talked about was cheating, identity theft, plagiarism, hacking, and other fascinating felonies.

"Actually, that would explain things," Maya was saying. "Maybe Zachary paid Imposter Boy to take his place."

"You think Imposter Boy would take my Spanish test tomorrow?" Olivia said.

"Sorry, he's busy," Maya said. "He's already taking Zachary's."

Okay, this conversation was officially becoming weird now. "Can we please talk about something else?" I begged. "Anyhow, who cares about Zachary Mattison?"

"Not Finley," Maya said. "Because she has a functioning brain."

"Not Maya," Hanna teased. "Because she's totally in love with Dylan."

"Untrue, actually," Maya said.

"Maya is over middle school boys," I explained.

Olivia laughed. "What does *that* mean?"

"No comment," Maya said, squinting off in the distance.

Olivia and Hanna turned to me, like I had some

big insight to contribute here, but I just shook my head. Because, honestly, I didn't.

"So, Maya," Olivia teased, "then in that case I guess you *don't* care that Dylan says he's coming to Chloe's party."

Maya glanced at me. "What party?"

"Oh," Olivia said. "You guys all know about it, right?"

"Remind us," I said.

"The one this coming Saturday night?" Olivia was smiling, but her eyes were panicky. "Chloe invited like the entire class."

"Right, that one." I gave Maya a look. "Yeah, it sounds sort of fun, but, unfortunately, we can't make it."

"Oh no! Why not?"

"Maya's brother is having this other thing, and he said we could come. So."

Maya's cheeks splotched pink. Her brother, Nick, was in eleventh grade at Fulton High, but all he ever did Saturday nights was play video games. So obviously he was not having *this other thing*, and even if he were, there was no way we'd be invited.

"Cool, a high school party," Olivia said, a little too enthusiastically. I could tell she didn't believe me.

Then Hanna's cell rang, some kind of Mozart-sounding ringtone. "Right, I'm on my way," she mumbled into her phone. She slipped the cell into her bag. "Sorry, you guys. Gotta go."

"Already?" Olivia said, pretending she was surprised Hanna was leaving.

"Major lesson. We're performing on Sunday, so I guess I can't make Chloe's party either." Hanna said it like she was apologizing to us, which was slightly, um, awkward. And not even necessary, since Hanna never went to parties. At least as far as I knew.

"Too bad," Olivia told her. "Well, have fun . . . practicing."

"I wouldn't call it *fun*," Hanna said, but she was smiling when she said it.

We watched her get into her mom's car. Mrs. MacPherson waved at us, we waved back, and then she drove off to Hanna's major lesson.

"The girl is obsessed," Olivia commented. "Obsessed."

That was when we heard Chloe's laugh, and saw her bursting out of the building with the following entourage: Jarret, Kyle, and Sabrina Leftwich. Jarret and Kyle were practically glued to her lately, and

Sabrina was her newest lapdog. Maya and I knew that Olivia had been Chloe's top lapdog just a few weeks ago, and that she and Sabrina were now competing for the so-called honor.

Maya gave me a pleading look.

"Well, so I guess we'd better take off too," I said casually.

"Really?" Olivia's eyes darted over to Sabrina, who was shaking her dark red hair and laughing way too loudly. "I think I'll hang out here another minute. I need to ask Chloe something."

"Hey, don't let us stop you." Maya yanked my arm. "Come on, Fin, I'm freezing."

"Don't forget, Finley, you're taking my picture tomorrow," Olivia called.

"Right," I answered. "When you aren't looking."

She stuck her tongue out.

"No really, I'm serious," I called over my shoulder. "It'll totally capture your essence."

Maya and I slogged through some grimy slush for about two blocks, not saying anything, my peacock-blue Keds getting soaked, my toes getting numb, my nose starting to drip.

Finally, Maya said, "So. Chloe's having a party."

"Yeah," I answered, sniffing. "Apparently."

"And *apparently* she invited, like, the entire grade."

"You don't know that, Maya."

"She invited Dylan, didn't she? Even after What Happened?"

Maya said this like I knew exactly What Happened, even though technically I wasn't there. Sure, I was *at* Chloe's day-after-Thanksgiving party, but when What Happened happened, I was sitting on the flowered sofa watching Ben Santino play Xbox. The truth was, parties like that had been excruciating for me ever since I fell out of crush with Kyle Parker. So I'd decided that maybe I wasn't giving certain boys a chance. Maybe it wasn't fair to remember them peeing on the rug in preschool or picking their noses on the school bus. Maybe I was doing that Fulton thing of focusing on one stupid detail from someone's personal ancient history, and then writing them off forever. I mean, boys were supposed to evolve, weren't they? That was the whole point of the *Amphibian Life Cycle*.

So there I was squished next to Ben Santino, trying to convince myself that he was a Croaker verging on Frogdom, that his hair wasn't greasy and he didn't still tease me about the way-too-short-bangs disaster and that he could possibly *have* a conversation about some topic *other* than the Green Bay Packers when suddenly we heard Chloe shriek.

Because (for some unknowable reason) she'd decided to step into the laundry room, where Maya and Dylan were sitting on a stack of towels, talking.

What Maya told me was that Chloe yanked the towels away and yelled specifically at *her* about respecting people's property—which probably meant the towels, because if it meant Dylan, that would just be too twisted. Because how could Chloe imply that Dylan was her personal "property"—even if, according to Olivia, she'd had a "secret crush" on him since sixth grade?

Anyway, the moral is, that was the last Chloe party we were invited to.

"And why am *I* being punished but not *him*?" Maya demanded. "How come she invited Dylan?"

"This is Chloe we're talking about, so who knows," I replied. "And don't forget, she didn't invite me, either."

"She didn't invite *you* only because of *me*." Maya tugged at the fringes of her scarf. "Chloe doesn't care about you, Finley. It's me she hates."

I sighed. "She doesn't hate you, Maya."

"She does. She *absolutely* does! You heard how she blamed me for that Spanish test tomorrow!"

"Yeah, that was unfair. And really unfair of Señor Hansen." Which made me sound like Zachary Mattison today at lunch, when he'd heard we had Hansen again for Spanish. *Not fair*, he'd said in an almost Tadpole way.

I immediately changed the subject. "And by the way, I can't believe you told the class about me taking photos."

"Why shouldn't I?" Maya argued. "I think it's awesome."

"But I have zero interest in boring yearbook photography! I mean, other than doing yours. And besides, I'm still learning how to work the camera."

"You're doing *amazing* with the camera! Remember that cartwheel shot you took at lunch?" Maya wiped her nose with a crumpled wad of tissue. "And anyhow, how did we get on this topic? We were talking about *Chloe*, and how she's trying to ruin my life."

A Fulton Middle School bus roared past us, spraying slush on all the cars. Out of an open window some fifth-grade uber-Tadpole was yelling, "YOU SUCK,

SUCKBRAIN!" And then another one stuck his head out and yelled, "SO DO YOU, SUCKBUTT!" Ah, boys that age. How charming.

"Oh, and did you catch all that cutesy 'I hate you' stuff with Olivia?" Maya asked, completely ignoring the display of gross Tadpole manners. "Since when did Olivia start talking like Chloe?"

"I don't know," I said. "They do hang out together, Maya. Like all the time these days."

"Which is insane! I mean, come on, Olivia isn't blind. Can't she *see* how nasty Chloe is? And spiteful? And power crazy?"

I shrugged. Because I'd learned that when Maya started ranting about Chloe, she wasn't really looking for answers. And truthfully, I'd never understood the whole Chloe mystique, anyway. So I'd never understood why Olivia had traded us in for Chloe.

When we got to Maya's street, she said, "Okay, Finley. So what about Saturday night?"

"What about it?" I asked doubtfully.

She smiled. "Are we going, or aren't we?"

"To the party?" I stared at her. "Of course not! We weren't invited."

Her smile shrank. She didn't answer.

"Maya," I said. "We *weren't*. And really, why do you even *want* to go? It's just going to be the same people, the same food, the same music—"

"The music isn't the issue, Fin."

"So what is? I mean, you really want to stand around eating cold pizza and watching Chloe spy on Dylan?"

This was kind of harsh on my part, but I was starting to feel nervous. "Besides," I added, "didn't you tell me at lunch today, 'Oh, I'm so beyond middle school boys, lalala'?"

She rolled her eyes. "Come on, Finley, you knew exactly what I was saying—I'm just sick of all the immaturity. And the point is, who's Chloe to decide what I do or don't do on Saturday? Who gave her that power?"

You did, I thought.

We crossed the street, where they hadn't picked up the garbage yet, so between the slush piles and the trash cans it was incredibly tricky to walk. Finally, we ended up in front of Maya's driveway.

I cleared my throat. "Um, listen, can I just say something?"

She shrugged one shoulder.

"Don't take this the wrong way," I said. "But seriously, Maya, nobody else makes you feel this bad. You're an incredibly strong person. So if Chloe tortures you all the time, why can't you just—"

"Look, it's a little hard to talk about."

This surprised me, because talking was always easy for Maya. Especially on the subject of Chloe. "So say it fast, all right?"

She didn't. She just stood there biting her chapped lip.

"Is it about What Happened with Dylan?" I asked.

"Not *just*. I really . . . don't think I can explain it very well."

"Come on, at least try."

"No," she said, squinting down the street. "What I mean is, I can't explain it *to you*."

Okay, maybe I wasn't hearing this right. Maybe there was some extra earwax in my ear. Also, I was wearing a thick wool hat. So possibly that was interfering with my ability to follow this conversation.

"Why not?" I asked, forcing a laugh. "Why can't you explain it to me?"

There was a long pause.

"Because it's about boys," she blurted.

CHAPTER 5

At first I did a *did you really just say that?* snort of disbelief. Then I managed to say, "*Excuse* me?"

Because you just don't let someone say that to you.

Not even your best friend.

"I'm so sorry," Maya said, touching my jacket sleeve. "I don't mean you don't get *boys in general.* Just that, you know, since you've never had *an actual date . . .*"

Unlike her, she meant. And Chloe. The only girls we knew who'd gone on official date-dates.

Even though Maya's barely counted, because the "dates" happened over the summer at gymnastics camp, and consisted of walking into town for ice cream like maybe four times with a ninth grader named Bryce.

A.k.a., Bryce Cream (my secret name for him).

But now Maya's *actual date* comment felt like a slap. And by the panicky look on her face, I was pretty sure Maya knew it.

So I decided to turn it into a dumb joke. "Acchhh," I said, frowning. "Vut iss dis *date zink* you speak of?"

"Ha ha." She wasn't smiling, though. "You're not mad at me for saying that?"

"Why would I be? I mean, hey, compared to you and Chloe and your vast dating experience—"

"Shut up." She was splotching pink, but giggling now.

"Because really, how could I possibly comprehend—"

"Okay."

"—the whole *concept* of boys in general—"

"*Okay, Finley.* I apologize. It came out all wrong, it wasn't what I meant, and you know I'd never, ever think that about you. I'm just upset about this stupid party."

"Well, don't be," I said. "Because it's just a stupid party."

"I know, I know! And I shouldn't obsess about Chloe, but . . ." She raised her eyebrows and clasped her hands in front of her mouth. "You forgive me, right?"

"Yes, of course." I grabbed my camera out of my jeans pocket and zoomed in on Maya's face. And . . . *click.*

She laughed. "What was that?"

"Your yearbook photo. You had a really interesting expression."

I showed it to her. It was a cross between hopeful and embarrassed, which was not a look she had often. Also, her hair was shiny.

"Kind of cool," she admitted. "Though maybe not for the yearbook. But thanks, Finley."

"You're velcome."

She threw her arms around me, squeezed tightly, and ran inside her house.

For a few seconds I just stood there, replaying the weirdness that had just happened.

Never mind, I finally told myself. Maya wasn't accusing me of *boy illiteracy.* She knew I was just sick of all the Tadpoles and Croakers we'd been dealing with since preschool. She was sick of them too; that's why she'd told me she was giving up on middle school boys.

And of course, Maya and I were doing the *Life Cycle* together, so it wasn't like she was noticing more boy stuff than I was. Frankly, lately I'd been writing most of the entries, doing the upgrades, keeping the chart in order. So she couldn't say I wasn't paying attention. Or that I didn't understand what I was seeing.

Also, she didn't mean she and Chloe were competing *about boys*. I was sure of that—Maya was smart and athletic; she had much better things to compete about. And competing about boys (even Froggy ones, like Dylan) was pathetic. And stereotypical. And a little bit twisted, too, if you asked me.

I slipped my camera in my pocket and began the slushy walk home.

When I opened the door, the front hall was crunchy. By that I mean that when I took off my Keds, I felt tiny, gritty chunks of something attaching themselves to my feet.

"NO!" I heard Addie shout from the kitchen.

"Just one bite," Mom was pleading.

"Nonono," Addie answered.

"But, Addie, you like this cereal!"

"No," Addie said. "*Hate* dis cereal!"

Silence.

"Okay, Max, then what about you?" Mom asked. Now her voice was perky and pretend-cheerful; she sounded crazed.

"NO," Max yelled. "BOOM!" Something clattered on the tiles, possibly a plastic sippy cup, which last week Addie had confirmed was tantrum safe.

I tiptoed past the kitchen, so that I wouldn't have to deal with the Terrible Two. But in addition to being "highly opinionated consumer experts" (Mom's phrase), my two-year-old twin siblings had super-hearing.

"Finneee!" Addie yelled. A different yell, a happy one. *Fiiinneeee!*

"Finley, is that you?" Mom called desperately. "We're in here!"

Dang.

I went into the kitchen. Max and Addie were sitting in recycled-plastic toddler seats shaped like cars (spearmint green for Addie, stop-sign red for Max), tossing fruit-sweetened Smiley-O's all over the tiles.

"Hey, guys." I kissed Addie's wispy hair and Max's sticky cheek. "How's the research going?" I asked Mom.

"It's not," she said, rubbing her temples.

I picked up three sample-size boxes of cereal, which had obviously been hurled from the plastic convertibles. "You shouldn't throw things, you two. Now look at the floor."

"Foo-wer," Addie agreed. She gave me a dimply smile.

Max hooted, steering his plastic wheel. "Gogogo!" he yelled so loudly I pulled my hat over my ears. "ZOOOM!"

"No yelling!" I yelled. As long as I was channeling Señor Hansen, I added the unibrow. But it just made the twins laugh hysterically and start pelting me with Smiley-O's.

"They're so fickle," Mom said. "Yesterday they ate nothing *but* Smiley-O's, and today they're just flinging it around. I don't know *how* I'm supposed to write a coherent review."

"You could say results were mixed," I suggested, removing half a Smiley-O from my big toe.

"Yeah, I guess I could, but readers like yes-or-no

opinions. Should I buy this overpriced product or not." She laughed tiredly. "Oh, and before supper I have to finish that podcast about double strollers; then I'm supposed to be taping an interview with the crazy anti-diaper guy. And how was *your* day?"

"The same. Although I have tons of homework."

She eyed me as she wiped Max's mouth with a wet paper towel. "Any tests coming up?"

"Just Boring Spanish."

"Ah," Mom said. "And may I remind you, *señorita*, on your last report card you had a D-plus in Boring Spanish."

I took a Granny Smith apple from the fruit bowl on the counter. "Because the teacher is evil."

"Because you don't study. You should let me help you, Fin, honey; I'm the queen of mnemonics."

I chomped on the apple. "Yes, but mnemonics aren't good for everything, Mom. They won't work for irregular-verb tests."

"Why not?" Mom argued. She wiped Max's face with the towel, then Addie's hands. "We'd have to be creative, but that's the fun part. Don't you remember how we used to drill your multiplication facts?"

I had to smile. Back in third grade, when I couldn't

remember eight times three, Mom came up with "I ate three donuts and barfed on the floor. Eight times three is twenty-four." When I couldn't remember six times six, she chanted, "Sticks times sticks is dirty sticks." I'd never be a genius at algebra, but for the rest of my life I'd probably always remember dirty sticks and donut barf.

Still, I couldn't imagine what good Mom's tricks would be for memorizing mindless conjugations like *tuve, tuviste, tuvo.* You might as well have to memorize bar codes or license plates.

And anyhow, it was my problem.

"I'll think about it, Mom," I promised. "But thanks."

She sighed. "All right. But Dad and I need to see a better grade this quarter, Finley. Or I'm afraid there'll be a consequence."

"Consequence?" I tossed the apple core. "What do you mean?"

"I mean," she answered, "something you won't be too happy about. Like maybe losing your camera for a month."

I almost choked on a piece of apple. My camera? But they'd just given it to me for Christmas. As a *present.* It seemed cruel and unfair to take back a *present,* especially one they knew I'd wanted since forever. And then to call it "losing" the present, as if the issue was I'd misplaced my new camera out of carelessness.

But I didn't argue with her, because what would have been the point? Losing my camera was obviously just a threat; it wasn't going to *actually happen.*

"Don't worry, I'll do great on this test," I told her.

"Well, I certainly hope so." Mom wiped her face with the dirty, sticky paper towel. "All right, Finny, since I can't help you with Spanish, you think you could possibly help me? I need a half hour, tops. If you could do your homework down here with the twins . . ."

"No problem."

"You sure?"

"I'll put on *Sesame Street.* Go work, Mom."

"Finny, you're awesome. Have I told you that lately?" She kissed my forehead and flew upstairs to be Mommy Oprah. Ever since the twins were born, Mom locked herself in her office every afternoon to do a blog called *Max 'n' Addie: 2 Cute 4 Words.* Plus a podcast called *Mommy & Us* ("all about raising gender-healthy multiples"). Plus toddler-junk reviews for *Chemical-Free Parenting* magazine, which is how the Test Twins got their lifetime supply of Smiley-O's.

It was weird—when I was little, Mom worked full-time at the local TV station, so basically I was watched by a bunch of babysitters. She switched to part-time when I was in elementary school, and even was troop leader for Green Girls, this exploring-nature group my friends and I did until seventh grade. But now she was home full-time as this uber-Mom expert-person, kind of a Frog version of a mom, if that was even possible.

The twins followed me into the TV room, where I switched on Elmo. He was learning to count pennies out loud, very slowly, lining them up on a picnic table in perfect rows.

"Nobody counts like that," I informed my siblings.

"Shh, Finnee," Addie scolded.

"Fine," I said. "Don't say I didn't warn you."

I plopped on the sofa with my science binder. I took out my chewed-up pencil and opened to the back, where we kept the *Life Cycle*. After what Maya had said to me about boys, I needed to read a few entries, to remind myself of my expertise on the subject.

First I turned to the latest update:

Wyeth Brockman: Tadpole with Croaker tendencies.

Okay, this status change still seemed right to me—not a full upgrade to Croaker, but fair. But now I needed to provide details, because you couldn't just upgrade someone without evidence.

I wrote:

Croaked on the word WEEKEND, blushed, and kinda/sorta asked Maya to stupid action movie. But still making bubbles through straw, still plays with LEGOs (need to confirm), chews thumbnail.

To be generous, I left extra space in case Wyeth had another growth spurt, even though something told me it wouldn't happen in the next twenty-four hours.

Then, to prove to myself I wasn't boy-illiterate, I skimmed some of the older entries on the chart:

Ryan Seederholm: Croaker. Smells like a gerbil. Why hasn't someone informed him about the invention of deodorant? Does he own any T-shirts WITHOUT references to superheroes? Talks like he has serious bronchitis.

<u>Jonathan Pressman</u>: Croaker. His voice sounds like a chain saw shutting off in slow motion. AAAaaagh. Also his hair is too long and his sleeves and pants are too short. Doesn't laugh-snickers and guffaws.

<u>Drew Looper</u>: Croaker. Upper-lip fuzz, visible in math (sits by the window). Not un-nice, but constantly cracking his knuckles. Video-game addict. Says "bro" and "dude," not ironically.

<u>Trey Gunderson</u>: Tadpole. Eats string cheese, brings a juice box from home. Giggles in science when we're studying "cell reproduction."

<u>Dylan McGraw</u>: RIBBIT!!! **(This was in Maya's handwriting.)** Compliments Maya's knitting (scarf)! Saves M a seat in the lunchroom! Laughs at M's joke! Gorgeous smile!!!

<u>Kyle Parker</u>: Croaker. Punches people in the arm for communication. Pizza stain on his football jersey. Can't breathe without

Jarret Lynch's permission. Frog potential, if he dumps Jarret. Maybe.

Ben Santino: Croaker. Hair grease, Xbox obsession, teases Finley about Bangs Fiasco. Incapable of non-sports-related conversation. Not un-nice, just un-Froggy.

Jarret Lynch: Croaker, although thinks he's a Frog. Follows Chloe around, laughs like hyena. Crams food into mouth, talks while chewing. Shoves, snickers, burps, grunts. Wears bad plaid.

Sam Knapp: Tadpole. Picks nose on school bus. End of discussion.

Cody Bannister: Tadpole. Carries Iron Man lunch box. Eats chocolate pudding. Super-squeaky voice.

Suddenly I remembered Zachary. Probably we'd never see him again after today, but he deserved mention in the *Life Cycle*, didn't he? Not just for the way he'd changed—because he was part of our class. Or used to be.

For a second I thought, *Oh, but wait, maybe first I should discuss this with Maya.* But I was still mad at her, I guess. And anyway, it wasn't like I needed her permission to write in my own notebook. Or to update the *Life Cycle*, which half belonged to me anyway. So I added:

> Zachary Mattison: Total Frog. Apparently skipped (hopped?) over Croaker. Didn't know you could do that, but

My cell rang; it was Olivia. The twins were mesmerized by a song about the joys of tooth brushing, so I went into the kitchen to answer in private.

"Guess what," she announced. Even though she hardly ever called me anymore, she didn't bother to say something like *Hey, Finley, it's Olivia;* she just started talking. "*Well.* After you guys left school today, I was with Chloe, and she was like, 'Omigosh, I feel so bad, because I didn't finish inviting all these people to my party.' So I said, 'You want me to make some calls for you?' And she was like, 'Would you? That would be awesome!'"

"Ah," I said. "And you're inviting us? For Chloe?"

"Obvi! I mean, I know you guys were planning to go to Maya's brother's thing Saturday night—"

"Yeah, we were."

"But just in case you'd rather be with your *class-mates* . . ." She paused. "And I told you, Dylan says he'll be there. Not that *you* care."

"Why wouldn't I?" After what Maya had just said to me about boys, it was a little hard not to overreact.

"Because Maya likes Dylan," Olivia explained. "And you like Kyle."

"Actually, I don't." See what I mean? People at Fulton filed away humiliating information and then tortured you for infinity. "Seriously, O, I haven't liked Kyle in like a year."

Longer than a year, but of course I wasn't about to launch into some big you'd-know-exactly-when-I-fell-out-of-crush-if-you-hadn't-dumped-us-for-Chloe speech.

"And speaking of Maya," I added, "I have no comment about Dylan, but *she's* specifically invited, right?"

"To Chloe's?" Olivia paused. "Why wouldn't she be?"

"Mmmf."

"Okay, I *know* there's a little weirdness between those two," Olivia admitted. "But we're all friends, aren't we? And Hanna also."

We were? I thought how extremely nice but also how strange it was that Olivia had this fantasy that nothing had changed since the Green Girl days, that we were still four best friends—but that off to the side, in a parallel universe, was Chloe. Or rather, Olivia and Chloe, plus Chloe's other assorted lapdogs.

"Then you guys will come to the party?" Olivia was asking.

"Not sure yet," I admitted. "Maybe."

"You have to! And by the way, I'm inviting Freakazoid."

"What?"

"Joking! Omigosh, Finley, could you imagine Chloe's *face*?"

Then she hung up.

Great, great, great. And now what was I supposed to do with this information? Go to Maya and be all like, *Hey, good news! Chloe says you're invited after all!*

Because, knowing Maya, she'd want the invitation straight from Chloe, not passed along from Chloe to Olivia to me, like we were first graders playing telephone. Plus she'd want an actual *invitation*—I don't mean all printed out like the Terrible Twos' birth announcements; I mean with Chloe looking her in the eye and saying, *Hey, Maya, I forgive you for the laundry-room incident with Dylan, and also for making Hansen give us a test tomorrow. Please come to my party.*

Really, the more I thought about it, the more I wasn't sure I should even tell Maya about this call.

But then I thought: *If I don't tell her, she'll want to crash the party. And maybe pick a fight with Chloe for not inviting her.*

Which Chloe did.

And also didn't.

"POW!" Max shouted so loud it sounded like a firecracker in my head. I spun around to see my little brother pointing a red rubber dolphin at me. "BOOM!"

"You should be watching Elmo," I snapped. "And stop pointing dolphins at people!"

"He's always pointing things and making sound effects," Mom announced, as she came into the kitchen with her empty mug. She put on the teakettle. "I think it's a gender thing, really, because Addie's more into people and language; you can talk to her; she's this little *person*. But boys." She smiled. "They're just so strange sometimes, don't you think?"

"Whatever," I said. "I have utterly no opinion about boys."

"You don't? Did something happen?" She lifted Max, kissing his messy curls.

Mom was clearly hoping for a heart-to-heart girl chat, but the last thing I felt like doing was telling her all about my supposed boy illiteracy. For one thing, it was kind of an excruciating topic; for another, if I told her, she'd probably ask a million follow-up questions. She might even end up calling Maya's mom. Besides, right at that second I was still processing the conversation with Olivia.

"Um, thanks," I said quickly, "but I actually do have a ton of homework."

"Yes, you said. But if you want to talk—"

"I NEED DOWN," Max protested, squirming out of Mom's arms and bolting down the hall.

The teakettle screamed. And somewhere in the house the phone started ringing.

Mom shot me a pleading look as she turned off the stove. "Finny, could you possibly answer that? I feel like my head is about to explode."

"No problem. Should I say you're here?"

"Oh, absolutely not! Tell whoever it is I've flown to Maui."

"Seriously?"

"All right, just say I'm working. No, wait—I'm in the shower."

What was weird at that moment was how young Mom looked, like a kid who hadn't done her homework. But at the same time she looked sort of old, her face all wrinkly, her hazel eyes crazy with tiredness.

"Okay," I said, searching the kitchen counter. "Where's the phone?"

"TV room, I think. Please hurry!"

I raced back into the TV room, almost tripping over a container of No Worries Organic Play-Clay. *Sesame Street* was still on, but Addie was sitting in the corner, calmly scribbling on the wall with a fat orange Crayola.

"Addie, what are you doing!" I scolded. "Naughty."

She burst into tears, so I scooped her up with one arm. Before I could stop her, she wiped goopy snot all over my shoulder. Lovely.

With my free hand I grabbed the phone from the sofa seat. It felt sticky, and I didn't want to know why.

"Hello?" I shouted over Addie's wailing.

"Finley?" a male voice asked.

"Yes?"

"Hi." There was a pause. "It's Zachary."

CHAPTER 6

I swallowed a huge gulp of air. Which might have
been helium, because when I spoke, my voice kind of
squeaked. *"Zachary?"*

"You sound shocked."

"Not at all! It's just that I couldn't hear very well."
I lowered Addie, who bolted toward the kitchen, still
bawling. "Um. Hi."

"Um hi back," he said.

It was funny how his voice sounded Froggier than
it had at school. Although come to think of it, I didn't
have scads of Frog experience on the phone. So possibly this was what they all sounded like.

Proof of my boy illiteracy? Gah, maybe.

Plus, now there was this awkward silence.

"Sooo," I said. "Was there any particular reason? Why you called?"

"Do people need particular reasons to call you?"

"No. Actually I get pointless phone calls all the time." Immediately I realized how wrong that sounded. But too late. "I just meant we haven't had a conversation in forever."

"We talked today at lunch. After I'm pretty sure you took my picture."

"I didn't take your picture!"

"Yeah? You were pointing your camera at me."

"Okay, maybe I was," I admitted. "But not to take your picture!"

"Then what for?" He was laughing. "Were you, like, spying on me, or something?"

I could feel my cheeks burn and my brain freeze up. Because what was I supposed to say here: *Fine, I confess: I was spying on your cuteness. But that was before I realized you were* you.

"Look, I'm sorry," I muttered. "It's just a new camera, and everyone keeps forcing me to take their photos. And I needed focus practice, and you were walking in the snow—"

"So you focused on me."

"Right. It could have been anyone, okay?"

"Oh, of course. No, no, I totally get it." He paused. When he spoke again, his voice sounded different. More serious. "And actually, Finley, I should apologize for teasing. Sometimes I overdo it."

"Well, exactly," I sputtered.

"Also, I think photography is a very cool hobby. I'm interested in learning more about it."

He was?

Oh.

"So am I," I said.

Awkward silence number two. And . . . still going.

"Anyway," he finally said in the nonteasing voice, "I guess I'll be seeing you tomorrow. Fisher-Greenglass said I could come back."

"Why would anyone stop you? You said you weren't expelled." As soon as this was out of my mouth, I wished I'd left out "you said." Because "you said" sounded as if I didn't believe him.

But if he thought I was accusing him of lying, he let it go. "Well, actually, I didn't leave school on the best terms with some people."

"Yes, I know," I said.

"So, yeah. And now I'm not . . . really sure what to

expect." His voice caught a bit on the word "expect." Almost a croak, but not quite. Then he added loudly and cheerily: "Anyhow, I believe in second chances, and I hope everyone else does too."

"Oh, they do, definitely," I lied.

"Awesome. Hey, Finley, I'm really glad I saw you today. Or rather that *you* were spying on *me*."

"Me too. Although I wasn't spying."

"Whatever," he said, and I could hear a smile inside the word. "Oh, and Finley? Don't forget your camera tomorrow. I'll let you focus-practice, if you want."

He hung up.

Well, that was strange, I thought. Not just the fact that Zachary had called me out of the blue, based on nothing but the camera incident, but also because of the odd, jumpy way he'd sounded. I couldn't put my finger on it, exactly, but it reminded me of Dad with the remote control, switching from channel to channel so fast it made me dizzy every time I watched TV with him.

Although to be fair to Zachary, he was probably feeling ubernervous about tomorrow. And how could he not be, I told myself, even if he hadn't been expelled?

But the call decided me. I now had two major

things to tell Maya: Zachary Mattison had called, and so had Olivia. The calls weren't related in any logical way, except that they both fell under the heading Reasons Finley Was Too Distracted to Do Her Math Homework.

And Reasons Why She Spent the Evening on the Internet.

And Ended Up Reading This Post on Her Mom's Blog:

Yesterday Max loved eating Smiley-O's, but today he only wanted to toss them all over my kitchen. Why? I think the simple answer is that he just enjoys watching things smash. To him this is funny—and even funnier when he adds sound effects, like BOOM.

As for Addie, her sense of humor—her sense of everything—is more sophisticated. Here's what I'm wondering—is it just my twins, or are toddler girls more complicated than toddler boys? Do they stay that way over time? (Thirteen-year-old Awesome Daughter is certainly a complicated person!) Am I making too much of the gender thing? Let me hear from you, friends. Comments below!

Xox,

Jen

• • •

I had to wait until the next day to talk to Maya, because Maya's mom was super strict about what she called "after-school socializing." According to Mrs. Lopez, afternoons were for homework and gymnastics practice, not for newsworthy phone calls from your best friend. Not for e-mails or texts, either. All of which, if you asked me, was a big reason why Maya obsessed so much about parties, and about weekends in general.

My plan was to get to school early on Tuesday, to meet Maya before homeroom. But that morning Dad insisted on making pancakes. He worked so hard running his car-parts company—"crazy busy" was how he described it—that it meant he missed most family dinners during the week. So when he decided to cook breakfast, you couldn't say, *No thanks, Dad, I'll just grab a bagel.* Besides, it was incredibly sweet of him to let Mom sleep late.

"Morning, Finster," he greeted me from the stove. "What's your opinion of blueberries this fine morning?"

"My opinion is, they're purple, not blue." This made me think of Zachary's eyes, which I didn't want to do. So I switched over to the comedy routine Dad had taught me when I was little: *"Why is there no blue food? I can't find blue food. I mean, green is lime; yellow is lemon—"*

"Orange is orange," Dad said, nodding.

"Red is cherry," I said, grinning. *"What's blue? Oh, they say, 'Blueberries!'"*

"Uh-uh," Dad recited. *"Blue on the vine, purple on the plate."*

Together we chanted, *"There's no blue food! Where is the blue food! We want the blue food!"*

Dad grinned as he handed me a plate of blueberry pancakes. "I can't believe you remember that entire George Carlin bit, Finster."

"Sure." I swirled some syrup on my plate and took a huge-ormous forkful of pancake. "Why wouldn't I?"

"Oh, I don't know. Because the human brain works in mysterious ways." He speared a pancake off my plate and chewed it thoughtfully. "Speaking of which, Mom mentioned you were having a bit of trouble memorizing Spanish?"

"Just irregular verbs. Because they're so random."

"So if they're tricky, why not let Mom help you? She's amazing at those memory things."

I rolled my eyes. "Yes, I know. She's the queen of mnemonics."

"And that's a good thing, right?" He took another bite.

"It's awesome. I'd just rather figure stuff out on my own."

"But why? If it's hard and she's willing to help you—"

"Dad, she's *willing,* but she doesn't have time. You should see her in the afternoons; she's practically mental when I get home. And anyhow, I can manage."

"I'm sure you can," Dad said, nodding seriously. "Nobody's doubting your ability."

Really? Then why did you and Mom threaten to take away my camera? I wondered.

He messed my hair. "Hey, Finster, wanna switch? You go to my office today and I'll go to eighth grade."

"Let me think about it," I said, kissing Dad's stubbly cheek with sticky lips. "See you tonight, okay? And thanks for the blue food."

As soon as I got to school, I raced to Maya's locker. About six weeks ago, before winter break, I'd decorated it for her as a birthday present, wrapping it in orange and hot pink paper, tacking rainbow-colored ribbons around the edges, taping up a collage of her favorite things—New York City, puppies, ice cream cones, the Olympic rings, fireworks. When girls decorated their best friend's lockers at our school, usually it stayed like that for a week or so. But Maya had kept my decorations, even though by now they were smashed and scraggly.

"Two news items," I informed her. "*Numero uno*, we're invited to Chloe's party."

She folded her arms across her chest. "We *are*? How do you know that?"

"Olivia called yesterday."

"Really? And she *said* we're both invited?"

"Officially."

"Huh," Maya said. "So in other words, *Chloe* didn't invite us. *Olivia* did."

See? I knew she'd pick up on this.

"But it still counts, right?" I argued. "You said you wanted to go. And now we don't even have to crash."

"I don't know, Fin. I was kind of psyched to crash. I kept imagining Chloe throwing one of her tantrums. While I stayed perfectly calm, of course." She squinted at me. "What's wrong with your tooth? It looks weird."

I ran my tongue over my teeth. Right away it hit something slimy: a tiny shred of blueberry skin. Eww, attractive.

I watched Maya take off a red wool scarf and fold it carefully, tucking it into a corner of her locker. "Okay," she said, "so what's *numero dos*?"

"Zachary called."

"WHAT?"

"Don't yell. Like fifteen minutes after Olivia."

"You're joking, Finley, right?"

"Why would I joke about that?"

"Why would he *call*?" She wrinkled her nose, like his call would smell bad.

"I don't know," I answered truthfully. "He's coming back to school today. He sounded pretty nervous."

"Yeah, well, he should be nervous. Considering what people think about him." She shook her shiny ponytail. "And anyway, Finley, why would he call *you*?"

That was a question I couldn't answer, even though I'd been thinking about it more or less nonstop since yesterday. But there was something about the fact that *my best friend* was asking it that made me feel, I don't know, a bit funny. Especially after that comment yesterday about me not comprehending boys.

"Why shouldn't he call me?" I asked her.

"Let me think. Because he was never your friend?"

"Maya, I don't think he was friends with anyone."

"Exactly my point. The boy was too Tadpole for the Tadpoles." She rolled her eyes. "Oh, who cares about Zachary. You brought your camera today, right?"

I nodded.

She did the *say cheese* grin. "Maybe at lunch we could try one more photo. I was thinking with the red scarf this time."

"The yearbook isn't in color," I reminded her.

"I'm perfectly aware. But red always makes me feel fabutastic." She batted her eyelashes at me like a demented Disney princess.

I started laughing but stopped when I saw Olivia rushing toward us, followed slowly by Sabrina Leftwich.

"You guys," Olivia cried, as soon as she was in front of Maya's locker. "Finley, I *know* we're supposed to shoot the photo today, but I woke up *totally deformed*—"

"You look fine," Maya insisted, squinting at Olivia's face.

"Check under my bangs." Olivia pulled back her hair. Sure enough, smack in the middle of her forehead there was a zit the size of a Lifesaver hole. Not hideous, but still.

"That's okay," I told her. "We have the rest of the week, don't we? That's plenty of time to outwit the Zit Gods."

Sabrina laughed through her nose. "The who?"

"Zit Gods," I said. "You know, the evil spirits who wreck yearbook photos—"

Maya shot me a look like, *Ack! Don't tell Chloe's lapdog about my zit photo!* Then she grabbed my arm. "Finley, omigod, look who's coming."

She pointed out Zachary, who was taking giant steps toward us. He was dressed almost exactly the same as yesterday—slouchy jeans, navy blue thermal, light gray hoodie. Except now he had an olive-green backpack slung over one shoulder.

I ran my tongue over my teeth to check for blueberry slime. Just in case.

"Hey, Finley," he said, smiling. "Hi, Maya. Olivia. Sabrina." He glanced at Maya's locker, then fixed his almost-purple eyes on me.

"You guys, isn't it great? Zachary's back at school," I said in this *rah-rah* sort of voice.

"Zachary?" Olivia squealed. "Omigosh, I didn't even recognize you! You've gotten so . . . *tall*."

Maya choked on a giggle.

"Yeah, I grew six inches in ten months," Zachary said. "Someone told me that's like a new world record. And none of my old clothes fit anymore, but the good news is, I'm working on my hook shot."

"I'm sorry, your what?" Olivia asked.

"Hook shot," I repeated. "That's a basketball term."

He grinned at me. "Finley, you know basketball?"

"She's on the girls' team this year," Maya said.

"Only as a sub," I explained. "And I barely get minutes. But Sabrina is our starting center."

Sabrina shrugged like *Please, no autographs.*

For a nanosecond my eyes met Zachary's. "I don't remember you playing basketball," I said. "I mean, before you left last year."

He looked away. "Yeah, well, unfortunately, I was always too short."

"Hey, watch what you say about short," Maya said, laughing.

Zachary smiled. "Oh, but it's different for girls. You guys are lucky. Nobody cares if you're short or tall or medium or whatever."

"That's not true," Sabrina said, glancing at Olivia. "You can't be a model if you're too short."

77

"Yeah, but models don't count; they're all cyborgs, anyway," Zachary said. "And besides, for gymnastics you're *supposed* to be small, right, Maya?"

Maya raised her eyebrows. "You remember I do gymnastics?"

"Sure. You're amazing. Didn't you win that championship, or something?"

"I made regional finals. On uneven parallels."

"And you had that photo in the paper."

"I looked awful. But yes. Wow, I can't believe you remember."

"I remember some things, but they're usually the wrong things; that's my problem. Well, one of them." Zachary ran his hand through his longish dark hair. "And I wasn't gone that long, although it feels that way sometimes. And now . . . the truth is, I'm not sure what to expect."

"Oh, I'm sure it'll be fine," Olivia said. But she said it in the loud, enthusiastic voice you use when you're telling your grandma how much you loved the sweater she knitted you for Christmas. And immediately Sabrina started pretend-coughing.

Zachary blinked. For a couple of seconds it seemed almost as if he'd lost his place in the conversation. Then he said, "Thanks, Olivia. I know I did some stupid things before I left. I'm just hoping people will give me a second chance."

The bell rang for morning homeroom.

"Okay, well," Zachary said. "I have to turn in some forms to Fisher-Greenglass, so. See you guys later, I guess."

He turned, and the four of us watched him disappear down the hallway.

CHAPTER 7

As soon as he'd turned the corner to the main office, Olivia and Sabrina raced off, probably to inform their fearless leader, Chloe.

But Maya didn't even seem to notice. "Do you think we should wait for him?" she asked me.

"Wait for who? You mean Zachary?" I stared at her. "Why?"

"I don't know. He seemed kind of nervous."

"Which *you'd* said wasn't surprising. Are you worried about him?"

"Maybe a bit," Maya admitted. "I mean, seriously, Finny, you know what it's like when people get this unfair *idea* about you. And how they can hold a grudge."

I couldn't argue. It was a Chloe reference, obviously, and you couldn't argue with Chloe references.

But Maya's reaction kind of surprised me. Ten minutes ago she'd been acting like his phone call smelled bad, and now she was volunteering to be his bodyguard? One more example of how unpredictable she'd been lately.

I flashed back to the time in seventh grade when Maya told Chloe that she was the one who'd invited Zachary to Chloe's party. Maya had defended him then, back when he was a Total Loser with sticking-out ears, so why was it weird she was defending him now?

It wasn't.

But somehow also it was.

We walked into homeroom. The second we took our seats, our English-slash-homeroom teacher, Ms. Richter, rapped on her desk.

"Okay, listen up, people," she said. "Some of you may be aware that a former classmate has returned to Fulton Middle. I know we'll all want to extend our warmest welcome back, and that I can count on you to behave graciously, like thoughtful, mature almost-high-schoolers."

Great, I thought. *If you call us mature, it's like practically daring us to act like toddlers.*

And then of course the entire class started buzzing.

So who's back?

Zachary Mattison.

Who?

You know. That annoying little jerk.

He's back? I hadn't noticed he was missing.

Did you see *him?*

You mean Freakazoid?

He's gotten sooo cuuute.

Okay, you're joking, right?

Zachary didn't show up for homeroom. But Maya and I were early for first-period science, and there he was in the front of the class, watching Mr. Lamott drink his Starbucks. That's what this teacher did all morning, slurp his Venti Americano, which was why we called him Mr. Coffee.

Maya grabbed my arm. "Come on," she murmured. "We need to do this."

"Do what?" I said, surprised.

She didn't answer. So I just followed her over to Mr. Coffee.

"Finley and I would like to be Zachary's lab partners," Maya announced. "He can borrow all our notes, and we'll get him caught up if he has any questions."

This was pretty much telling Mr. Coffee that we'd do his job for him, so how could he refuse? Especially considering how brilliant Maya was at science and also how much he hated to teach.

"Sounds like a plan," he said, exhaling coffee vapor all over us.

Zachary flashed a smile. He followed Maya and me to our lab station in the back of the classroom.

"Thank you," he said. "You didn't have to do that."

"No kidding," Maya answered, laughing. "Do *not* make us regret this. Right, Finley?"

"Yup. Right," I said, not looking at either of them. I opened my lab notebook and started filling in one of the graphs.

And I guess that was sort of hostile on my part, but I was kind of rattled by the whole arrangement. Maya hadn't even asked me if I was comfortable being Zachary's lab partner; she'd just gone ahead and signed us both up. And I wasn't *against* it, specifically; I just felt decided for.

Plus there was the whole Maya-changing-her-mind-on-me issue.

Plus, and I know this will sound lame, but sitting next to Zachary was going to be super distracting. Science was my least-good subject, even worse than Spanish, and the last thing I needed was something to take my mind off the human respiratory system, or the insides of a cell, or whatever fascinating topic we were exploring that day. And with Zachary on the lab stool between Maya and me, I knew concentrating would be impossible.

So the way I dealt with all of this was by not dealing. Avoiding eye contact, hunching over my lab notebook. Scribbling.

But I wasn't taking lab notes. I was taking mental notes. And here is what I observed about my new lab partner:

1) He was a foot tapper. Zachary spent that entire period tapping his foot under his desk. Not like one or two taps either—a whole percussion section worth of taps. I wondered if the foot-tapping thing was something new, maybe caused by first-day-back-at-school nerves. Or maybe he was just a nervous person, despite the sudden Frogginess.

2) He had a freckle on his neck. No comment about the freckle; it was just this random thing I noticed.

3) His clothes smelled like laundry detergent. What

was interesting about this was that Zachary was wearing almost the identical outfit yesterday, so obviously he'd washed his clothes and put some of the same stuff back on today. This struck me as bizarre, especially for a Frog—but on the other hand, my little brother Max wore his *Toy Story* shirt straight out of the dryer, so not rotating your wardrobe was possibly what Mom called "a gender thing."

4) Zachary had something written on his wrist in tiny black uppercase letters. I didn't get a good look, but I was pretty sure it said "LUNCH."

And of course as soon as I noticed that—*LUNCH*—I couldn't think about anything else. Why would someone write "lunch" on their own skin? To remind himself to eat lunch? Or to remind himself to do something *during* lunch?

Like what, for example?

Spy on *me*?

No, I told myself. *Don't be ridiculous, Finley.*

The rest of that morning, I kept my distance from Zachary. But I couldn't stop spying on him, even without my camera, which I'd left in my locker for safekeeping.

It was so strange—everything about this boy seemed like the opposite of the old Zachary Mattison. It wasn't just that he didn't make obnoxious jokes or fall off his chair; it was almost as if he'd been reprogrammed to be Froggy. Like the old Tadpole model had been returned to the store, and someone had erased all the data on his hard drive.

Because, I mean, Zachary was definitely cool now. Even with the foot tapping and the laundered clothes and the mysterious *LUNCH* logo on his wrist.

And he was especially cool with girls. The boys weren't sure about him—I could see the Tadpoles stealing looks, and the Croakers pretending to ignore him—but the girls who spoke to him (for example, Olivia, who shared a work station with him in social studies) seemed mesmerized by every word he said. Zachary asked questions; he listened to answers; he made almost-purple-eye contact; he smiled. Really, he wasn't just Froggy compared to the old Zachary. He was Froggy compared to the Frogs.

Which I suppose qualified him for the category Prince. That is, if there even were such a category. It suddenly occurred to me that there should be: Boys wouldn't stop evolving at Frog, would they? At least, they kept on evolving in fairy tales. But I couldn't decide on this by myself; obviously, I needed to discuss this important question with Maya.

Although for some extremely mysterious reason he still needed a reminder about *LUNCH*.

At lunch it was face-hurting cold again, but Maya promised she'd pose really fast. And after the way I'd sulked through science, I felt as if I owed her a year-book photo shoot. So we each grabbed a microwaved pizza bagel in the cafeteria and then headed outside to the snowy field.

That day a crusty layer of ice had formed over the snow, which crunched under our feet. When we got to a spot where there was a patch of sunlight, Maya flung her red scarf around her shoulders, wiped her drippy nose with her ungloved finger, and announced, "All right, Fin, this is perfect."

But she seemed distracted. As I experimented with the lens, she kept biting her chapped lips and squint-ing past me, at the lunchroom doors.

"Are you cold?" I said. "We could just do this inside."

"No, then everyone would watch, and I'd be

self-conscious," Maya said. "Just hurry and take the picture, Finley, okay?"

I zoomed in and out, but there was no point. If someone wants to look fabutastic, they need to concentrate on fabutasticness.

"Okay, something is wrong," I declared. "Did Chloe say something to you?"

"No, she didn't even talk to me today. Which is strange, since she quote-unquote invited me to her party."

I sighed, fogging up the lens. "What is it, then?"

"Nothing. I don't know. You'll think I'm crazy."

"I already think you're crazy."

"Ha ha." But she wasn't smiling. "Okay, fine. I invited Zachary to join us."

"You mean *now*?"

She nodded.

Ah, I thought. Well, that explained *LUNCH*. He didn't want to forget Maya's invitation, so he wrote himself a note on his wrist.

"Why did you invite him?" I said, pretending to fuss over the camera.

"Two reasons. One, I didn't want him to be sitting all by himself in the cafeteria."

"Maya, I doubt he'd be alone," I said. "Didn't you notice Olivia with him in social studies? They were being incredibly friendly with each other."

"Yes, they were," she agreed patiently, as if she'd thought about that before. "But Olivia usually sits with Chloe at lunch, and I don't trust how Chloe will react. She was always so horrible to Zachary, remember? I'm positive she'll hold a grudge. And of course there's the dread Sabrina. Also, people wander around the cafeteria, and what if someone like Jarret comes over to pick a fight?"

I shrugged. The truth was, I'd been thinking a Zachary-Jarret confrontation was inevitable, and probably soon, but I'd been wondering about Chloe. You'd think Zachary was the sort of Froggy Frog she'd totally approve of now. But there was the grudge issue. Although possibly Maya was making way too much of it.

"What's the second reason?" I said.

"Okay. Finley, don't you think it would be awful to be the only eighth grader without a photo in the yearbook? I mean, without even a candid shot?"

I looked up from the camera. "Maya? And you're volunteering *me* for this assignment?"

She didn't answer.

"You *already* volunteered me?" I said.

"Only because I knew you'd want to! You're shooting Olivia—"

"Because she begged me. And we used to be friends."

"You're sort of friends with Zachary, too, now, aren't you? He called you yesterday."

"That wasn't friendship. That was . . ." But I didn't know what it was. Channel surfing, or something.

"Look, if you really don't want to," Maya said.

"I didn't say that, Maya. I just wish you'd asked me first."

"Sorry." She wrapped the scarf around her like a shawl. "But I was only trying to help."

And I thought: *Help who? Help with what?*

Suddenly Maya started waving frantically "Over here!" she shouted to Zachary, who was standing by the cafeteria door.

I watched him across the snowy field. For a second or two he hesitated; then he started loping toward us. His walk reminded me of some animal, but I couldn't think which one. A jaguar? No, jaguars were probably fast, and Zachary wasn't fast. Just sort of . . . lopy.

Did frogs lope? No, they hopped. Loping and hopping were completely different actions. And I shouldn't think of him as anything but an amphibian, because the *Life Cycle*—anyhow, *his* Life Cycle—was confusing enough without bringing in mammal behavior.

By then he was in front of us, his cheeks flushed from the cold.

"I was starting to think you'd forgotten!" Maya shouted at him, laughing.

"Not likely," I commented.

Zachary blinked at me. "What do you mean?"

"You wrote yourself a reminder. You know. On your wrist."

"What are you talking about?" Maya demanded.

"Zachary wrote *LUNCH* on his wrist," I explained, feeling totally moronic right then, like I was tattling on him.

He immediately stuffed his hands inside the front pocket of his hoodie. "No I didn't," he muttered.

My mouth dropped open. "You did, too. I saw it!"

"That's not what it says, okay?"

"It's not? What does it say, then?"

"Nothing." He could have shown me his wrist at

that point, to prove that I'd been hallucinating. Except he didn't. Instead he stared right into my eyes, like he was trying to hypnotize me.

So I stared right back.

And when he refused to blink, I knew he was lying.

"Hey, Finley, it's freezing out here," he finally said. "Do you only take photos in the snow?"

"Of course not," I answered. By then I'd turned away, but my heart was pounding.

He's lying.

Why is he lying?

He smiled at me. "That's a relief. Can we please go inside now?"

"Sure," Maya said. My eyes met hers, and I realized she'd been watching me, trying to read my mind. "We can go to the gym for the rest of lunch. Maybe shoot some hoops?"

Hoops? Since when did Maya start playing basketball?

"Yeah, great," Zachary said. "I'm working on my hook shot."

"Yes, you told us this morning," I pointed out.

Maya made a face at me like, *Shut up, Finley, what is your problem?* And the three of us crunched our way back indoors without talking.

• • •

As soon as we were back inside the overheated building, Zachary announced that he had to "deliver some papers" to Fisher-Greenglass, even though he'd already given her a bunch of "papers" before homeroom. Then Maya said she was on the verge of frostbite and didn't feel like finishing her photo session, which was seriously fine with me.

The truth was, I was starting to feel as if the photography thing was getting out of control. It was one thing to take your best friend's picture as a favor so she wouldn't be stuck with a zit photo in the yearbook, but now I was expected to take not only Olivia's picture but also Zachary's. Which would be awkward enough under normal circumstances. My best friend obviously liked him, and as for me, I had a majillion thoughts about Zachary Mattison all swirling around, like my head was a snow globe. Maybe I liked him, maybe I didn't. I definitely thought something was a little bit off about him. And one thing I knew for sure: Now that I'd accused Zachary of lying about the *LUNCH* tattoo, a photo shoot with him would be excruciating.

Also, this was another instance of being decided-for by Maya, the second one that day. And I needed to be by myself to calm down, or we'd probably be heading for a fight.

So when Maya said she'd just go back to the cafeteria until lunch was over, I decided to go to the school library. It was always soothing in there, and the librarian, Ms. Krieger, was awesome. One time in September when I had cramps, the school nurse wouldn't let me miss gym, so I went to the library and "helped Ms. Krieger with a research project." At least, that's what the note said that Ms. Krieger wrote to my gym teacher.

Now she was studying me over her lime-green glasses. "Finley, you look frozen. Would you like some hot chocolate? I have the kettle on in my office."

See? Awesome.

"Thanks," I said. "Actually, I wanted to look at some camera books. Do you have any?"

"But of course," she said in a pseudo-French accent that made me giggle. I didn't always understand her strange sense of humor, but she was definitely my favorite grown-up at Fulton Middle.

Ms. Krieger walked over to a shelf near the windows. "Here are all the technical guides. I like this one: *Amazing Face: How to Reveal Character with Your*

Digital Camera. Over here are books of photos. You should look at both types of books, because it's not just about pressing buttons; you want to develop your eye. Are you into landscapes or portraits?"

"Portraits. Definitely."

"Ahh. This gives me no surprise. You strike me as a student of character, Mademoiselle Finley."

I laughed. "I do?"

"Mais oui."

"But how can you tell that?"

"Because, *ma cherie, je suis une* stud-ent of char-act-aire, too."

She started piling books into my arms—thick, glossy collections of portraits by people named Annie Leibovitz, Richard Avedon, Irving Penn, Diane Arbus, Yousuf Karsh. Then she sat me on her squishy red sofa and disappeared to check on her kettle.

For the rest of lunch period I flipped through pages of faces—some were famous, glamorous people I recognized, or semirecognized; some were just normal people with wrinkled foreheads, stubbly chins, and bad haircuts. A lot of the shots were posed in studios, but some were taken on the street, in cars, on balconies, in alleys—candid shots catching people by surprise, I guessed. And all of the photos made you wonder: What was the person thinking at that second? Or feeling?

Mostly you could tell right away. But sometimes the answer seemed mysterious, complicated, hidden behind their eyes, or underneath their skin.

CHAPTER 8

When lunch ended, Ms. Krieger suggested I check out a few of the books, so I picked two volumes of portraits— one by Annie Leibovitz, one by Richard Avedon—and the how-to book called *Amazing Face*. But they were too heavy to lug around all afternoon, so I crammed them into my locker, then ran upstairs to Spanish. By then I was already a minute late for the full-period test. And I knew this meant Señor Hansen would humiliate me before I could even pick up my pencil.

But when I opened the door to Spanish, instead of seeing everyone hunched over their tests, I walked in on Zachary standing by the whiteboard.

Hairy Hands barely even noticed me as I slipped into my seat. This was because he was laser-focused on Zachary.

"Well, this was unexpected," Hairy Hands was grumbling. "I hadn't planned on a new student arriving in the middle of eighth grade."

"I'm not new," Zachary said flatly. "I'm just back."

"Well, you're new to our room, and you're new to our curriculum. And I suppose you'll be needing a desk." He said this as if desks were something Zachary had invented just to be inconvenient.

"Mr. Hansen, Zachary can sit next to me," Maya called from the back of the room. "I'll help catch him up."

It was the same win-win offer she'd made in science. But Hairy Hands wasn't as lazy as Mr. Coffee.

"Thank you, Señorita Lopez, I'll keep that in mind. But I've arranged the desks to maximize conversational opportunities." He unibrowed the room. "Señor Mattison, please take the seat next to Señorita DeGenidis."

"No!" Maya blurted out.

The room gasped.

"Excuse me?" Señor Hansen said. He crossed his hairy arms.

Maya's cheeks splotched pink. "I just mean, I don't think that would be a good idea. For Zachary."

"Why not?" Chloe spun around to face Maya. "You think you're the only decent student in this class?"

"No, that's not what I—"

"You always have to be the best at everything, don't you, Maya. Nobody else gets to do anything. Only you."

"Girls," Señor Hansen said. "That's enough now."

Maya ignored him. "Chloe, *what* is your *problem*?"

"My problem?" She looked at Sabrina like, *Did she really just say that? "My* problem?"

"Right. Your problem. Ever since Halloween."

"*Girls,*" Señor Hansen warned.

"You don't actually expect me to answer in front of the entire class, do you?" Chloe said. "Because seriously, Maya, I will."

My heart was pounding. I knew I couldn't just sit there and watch my best friend get humiliated while Chloe described What Happened in the Laundry Room to the entire class. I had to stop this scene, or at least provide a distraction.

"Zachary can sit next to me," I announced loudly. "There's an empty desk right here." I pointed to the scratched-up, wobbly-legged desk across from mine.

"Or he can move it over here," Olivia said. "There's plenty of room."

"Ooh, Zacha-wee, sit over here," Jarret said in this fake high-pitched voice. He clasped his hands and batted his eyelashes. "Pweeeese."

So then of course Kyle started guffawing. And immediately, a bunch of other Croakers started squealing, "Ooh, Zachary, sit here, sit here."

I glanced at Zachary. His face was flushed and he was smiling, but I could tell it was forced.

"Shut up, all of you," Maya ordered. "This isn't preschool, all right? Mr. Hansen, why *can't* Zachary sit next to Finley?"

Chloe gaped at Sabrina. "I don't believe this. Now Maya's assigning seats? Señor Hansen, she's out of control!"

"Maya and Chloe," Señor Hansen said through his teeth. "If either of you say *one more word*, you're going straight to Ms. Fisher-Greenglass."

"Okay, sorry," Maya said quickly.

For a second the room was quiet.

Then she added: "Although I *really* think he should sit with Finley."

It was strange. Señor Hansen was evil, and also a terrible teacher, but at that moment he reminded me of Mom—crazy tired, trying desperately not to lose it, even while Smiley-O's were flying past his head from all directions. You could see his jaws clenching and his hairy hands trembling as he mentally scrolled through the Fulton Middle School Code of Behavior.

"All. Right," he said. "That is *way* more than enough. Maya—Señorita Lopez—go march yourself to the principal's office."

"Me?" Maya's mouth dropped open. "Why just me? Chloe was arguing too!"

"You mean defending herself," Sabrina insisted.

Maya glared. "Sabrina, mind your own—"

"Maya, don't talk," I said loudly. "Just go. Now. Please."

Maya turned to me, her eyes flashing. "Thanks for your support, Finley," she snapped.

She flung her red scarf over her shoulder, grabbed her backpack, and ran out of the classroom.

Hairy Hands sank into his teacher chair. "The rest of you open your blue books. As some of you may remember, this is a class, not the Roman Colosseum, and we're due for a verb test."

"But we won't even have a full period," Olivia protested.

"That's hardly my fault, is it, Señorita Moss? And why are you still standing there?" he thundered at Zachary.

"I'm not . . . sure where to sit," Zachary said.

"Just sit wherever you want. We've wasted way too much time on this issue!"

Zachary took the empty desk next to me. I was too upset to look at him, so I just opened my blue book. And while I filled the pages with conjugations, or what I imagined were conjugations, out of the corner of my eye I could see Zachary drawing robots.

"Oh, Hanna, it was totally awful," Olivia exclaimed at dismissal, as we stood on the steps waiting for Maya. "Maya went completely mental on Chloe."

"Actually, Chloe went mental right back," I said.

"Because she had to," Olivia insisted. "Maya was attacking her in public. She couldn't just sit there and not say anything! And then the way Maya turned on *you*—"

"She was just upset, okay?" I didn't want to think about what Maya had said to me before she left the classroom, and I definitely didn't want to discuss it with Olivia. Who, I had no doubt, would go reporting back to Chloe. "Hanna, did you notice Maya in orchestra?"

"No, but I wouldn't," Hanna said. "I'm viola section; she's oboe."

I nodded impatiently. Of course I knew what instrument my best friend played; to be honest, I always thought her oboe sounded like a goose with cramps. But I never told Maya that, because even though she wasn't as music-obsessed as Hanna, she worked hard at it. Hard at everything. Which is why she was a super student, and never, ever got in trouble.

"I'm just worried," I said. "I haven't seen her all afternoon."

"Maybe Fisher-Greenglass gave her detention," Hanna said. "I mean, really, Finley, talking back to *Hairy Hands*—"

Olivia said, "Yeah. I don't think I've ever seen him that mad."

"Me neither," I admitted.

"Oh, but she'll be fine," Olivia said quickly. "Maya is fierce. And anyhow, it was cool how she yelled at Jarret and the rest of those morons."

She fluttered her hand at the boys who were standing by the doors. Ben Santino and three other Croakers were shoving each other like they'd just sprouted Croaker arms and didn't know what else to do with them. They were all laughing—rude, croaky guffaws—and when Ben Santino pushed Jonathan Pressman, I could see Zachary standing in the middle. Right next to Jarret and Kyle.

My stomach twisted. What was happening? Were they ganging up on him?

No, Zachary was grinning.

Which was weird all by itself.

And then this happened: Jarret gave him a fist bump.

Jarret.

Gave Zachary.

A fist bump.

"So, Finley," Olivia was saying. "If I don't look hideous tomorrow, can we please take my photo? Sabrina keeps warning me about this Friday deadline thingy."

"Sure, no problem," I answered. But I wasn't listening. What was Zachary grinning about? And why was he being fist-bumped—not bullied, not even teased—by Jarret Lynch? Of all people?

I watched Hanna run off to her mom's car, and Olivia run off to join Chloe. And then I sleepwalked back into the gym for basketball practice, even though I couldn't concentrate on layups.

Because here is what I kept thinking: While Maya had gotten into big trouble trying to protect Zachary, he'd gone off and become a Croaker hero. Or something.

Based on what?

I couldn't imagine. The Croakers had ignored him before today in Spanish. And in Spanish, what had happened, anyhow? Zachary had basically just stood there; the whole class was Maya versus Chloe.

I didn't get what they suddenly saw in him. Although really, the more I thought about it, I didn't get much on the subject of Zachary. What he'd said about wanting another chance—well, you couldn't argue with it. People deserved second chances. Except there was something about the way he kept repeating it all the time. That just seemed weird to me, almost as weird as his Froggy makeover. Or metamorphosis, or whatever you wanted to call it.

And then there was that weirdness about the

LUNCH tattoo: not just writing it on his wrist, but lying about it.

And talking constantly about his hook shot; that was weird, too.

I mean, if you started thinking about it, there was a ton of weirdness about this boy. Enough for an entire chart.

CHAPTER 9

When basketball practice was over, I didn't go straight home. I told myself that I was just taking the long way, stretching my legs, lalala, but the truth was, I was heading over to Zachary's house.

I wasn't sure why. I just knew that I needed some answers. Maybe, I thought, if I walked past his house, I'd notice something—even a small, random thing— that would help solve the mystery of Zachary Mattison.

From trick-or-treating routes our Green Girls troop had mapped back in the fifth grade, I remembered that his family lived somewhere on Spruce Street. But I didn't know exactly where, and it was a long, busy block full of snowball fights and squirrels and mini-vans backing up out of driveways and ladies in down jackets pushing strollers. I didn't want to peep at everyone's mailboxes to search for the name Mattison. And I didn't want to walk over to one of the stroller-pushing moms to ask which house was his, in case afterward she blabbed *(Oh, Zachary honey, this tall, pool-noodle-shaped girl with freckles and boring brown hair was searching the entire neighborhood for you. . . .)*.

So I took out my camera. I pretended that I was taking street pictures for the school newspaper, which all the teachers called *The Bugle* and all the kids called *The Bug*. And I walked up the west side of Spruce Street, snapping photos of garbage cans and fire hydrants, but in reality searching for clues about Zachary's whereabouts.

I did this for about five minutes, until I heard someone shout my name.

"Finley? What are you doing here?"

My heart stopped.

Then I realized it wasn't Zachary; it was Wyeth Brockman, the almost-but-not-quite Croaker, the one who'd told Maya he was seeing that stupid movie, *Battlescar III.*

"You're taking pictures," he announced. "What for?"

"None of your business," I muttered.

Wyeth smiled. His face was two-thirds braces, so when he did this smile it was basically wire. I'm pretty sure that back when I wore braces, you could see actual teeth. "This is my block." he said. "So I think it is my business."

"Fine." I sighed. "I'm taking pictures for *The Bug*."

"Of fire hydrants?"

"Of our town. They're doing a . . . two-page spread about Spruce Street."

"That would be sort of boring, wouldn't it? Two entire *pages*?"

I looked at him. Not only was Wyeth tiny, he was stick skinny, and his hair was poofy on top. Really, he resembled a Q-tip. If a Q-tip had braces, and desperately needed a haircut.

On the other hand, *he was talking to a girl*. His voice wasn't croaking, or anything, but this was Croaker behavior. A Tadpole mutating before my eyes.

I heard the camera turn off. "Yeah, I guess it would be boring. Although doesn't anything interesting ever happen on this street? Like new people moving in? Or moving back? Or something?"

He thought for a second. "Nah. At least, I can't remember anything like that. But I could give you a tour, if you want."

"You mean of the block?"

"Yeah. You know, for the newspaper."

Okay, I thought. Here was my chance to find out some information about Zachary Mattison. And I didn't even have to ask for it—Wyeth was offering to help. In a very nice, polite, almost Froggy way, actually.

I made a mental note to update his status on the *Life Cycle: Wyeth Brockman, Croaker.* Because even if it looked funny on paper, it was true.

But I couldn't walk with him. I didn't want to have to chat about boy movies I'd never see. Also, I was pretty sure he had a crush on Maya.

Plus, I know this sounds stupid, but I didn't want to risk Zachary looking out of his window, spotting me walking around with Wyeth, and getting some bizarre, warped idea about the two of us.

So I thanked Wyeth for the offer. And ran.

When I got home, Mom was in the kitchen with her laptop and a steaming mug with a picture of the Wiggles on it.

"How was your day?" she asked.

"Oh, you know," I said. "Basketball practice. Spanish test."

"Ah, *sí, señorita*. And how did that go?"

"It went." I grabbed an apple off the counter and took a loud, juicy chomp before Mom could threaten anything about my camera. "Where is everyone?"

"Napping, thank goodness. I tried giving them a bath together after lunch, and it was a disaster. Addie was okay, but between you and me, if I had to listen any more to Max's wild rumpus—"

I rolled my eyes. "Seriously, Mom. He's such a Wild Thing now."

"Because he's a boy, Fin, honey. They're all like that when they're two."

"But they grow out of it, right?"

She sipped some tea from the Wiggles cup. "Oh, definitely," she insisted. "Look at Dad."

What a random thing to say, I thought. Dad was like another species compared to Max. Or to the guffawing, shoving, fist-bumping Croakers at school.

I mean, Dad woke up early to make us *blueberry pancakes*. That wasn't even a category of amphibian.

• • •

Inside my room I yanked off my stinky gym clothes. Then I flopped on my bed, and took out my science binder.

The *Life Cycle* needed an update.

Wyeth Brockman: Croaker. Still looks like teeny Tadpole, and hasn't croaked since the word WEEKEND. But talking to girls (specifically, Finley), making eye contact, just offered a neighborhood tour . . .

Although the tour offer was definitely Froggy, so maybe it didn't belong in a description of Croaker behavior. Wyeth was sort of a mess, I thought—all three stages at the same time, a Croaker with Tadpole and Froggy qualities, like one of those half fish/half frog mutants showing everything at once: tail, arms, legs. He wasn't even a specific species at this point; he was just a skinny little blob of amphibian.

But at least he was making forward progress. As opposed to Zachary—who was a Frog (or a more-than-Frog) but who now was hanging with the Croakers. And not just hanging with—fist-bumping and laughing. What did that mean? Was that like doing the *Life Cycle* in reverse? Unevolving?

Could you even do that? I didn't know reverse evolving was technically possible.

"BAMPOW," Max shouted from outside my closed door. "I'M THE COPS."

Great, I thought. *Let the wild rumpus begin.*

"Max, I'm doing homework; be quiet," I yelled.

Quick footsteps, then a few frantic knocks on my door.

"Finny." It was Mom. "Could you get the kitchen phone, please?"

"It's ringing? But I'm changing my clothes."

"Okay, but Addie's on the potty and I can't leave her by herself. Could you please just throw on a robe and hurry?"

First I groaned uberloudly through the closed door; then I grabbed my bathrobe and ran downstairs to the kitchen. Maybe it was Maya, I told myself, sneaking a call to tell me she'd survived detention. And wasn't mad at me for telling her to stop arguing with Hansen. And was sorry she'd been all snippy at me. In public.

"Hello?" I said hopefully.

"Finley? It's Zachary."

"Why?"

"Oh." He sounded confused. "Am I interrupting? I could call back—"

"No. I mean, why aren't you calling Maya?" I said this thinking that Maya was possibly still in detention. But even if she'd been freed, and was back home by now, her mom wouldn't let her talk on the phone during homework time. Especially not if she'd gotten punished by the principal.

So why had I asked him that? I had absolutely no idea. Except for the fact that it made no sense he was calling *me*.

"You got Maya in massive trouble today," I added.

"Yeah, I know," Zachary said in his serious voice. "I feel really bad about the whole thing. Even though I don't think Maya's fight with Chloe was *my* fault."

He was right; it wasn't. But that was *so* not the point. "You should still thank her," I insisted.

"I will, Finley. And I also wanted to thank *you*."

"Me?" I said, surprised.

"You know. For offering that desk."

"I only did it to help Maya. Not that it worked." My heart was speeding up, so I took a breath. "Zachary, can I please ask you something? At dismissal you were hanging with all those guys. Jarret, Kyle, Ben—"

"Yeah. Kind of."

"And I heard laughing. What was it about?"

"Nothing," he said fast.

"Not about Maya?"

"No way. They wouldn't, Finley. I think they're all scared of her, actually."

Well, that was certainly believable, I thought. Maya could be pretty scary. "So what was so funny, then?" I said.

"Finley, it's stupid."

"Tell me anyway."

"No, I mean it's *really* stupid."

"Zachary, will you please just *talk*?"

"Okay." He cleared his throat. "So. Apparently they thought it was hilarious that all these girls would be fighting over my desk. Not that you *were*, but."

Oh, great, great, great. Croakers were laughing *about us. About me.*

But I couldn't let Zachary know how humiliating this felt. "Well, thanks for that news flash," I said with fake cheeriness. "I'm glad we were all so entertaining. And I'm glad you're making friends with Jarret."

"I wouldn't call him a *friend*."

"Whatever he is. At least you're not fighting any-more."

"Yeah, that's true, I guess." I could hear Zachary breathing. Then in a voice with just the faintest detect-able crack in it, he said: "Anyhow, I just called to say thank you, Finley. For the desk. And also, you know, for giving me a second chance."

CHAPTER 10

The next morning I got to school super early so that I could be sure to have time for a private one-on-one talk with Maya. Apparently she'd made the same plan, because when I got there, she was sitting next to her locker, trying to retape a rainbow ribbon that was dangling off my birthday decorations. As soon as she saw me, she sprang up and gave a quick, sharp hug.

"So what happened yesterday?" I said. "Are you okay?"

"Ish." She did a wince-smile. "Fisher-Greenglass gave me a two-day in-school suspension, so I'm stuck in the computer lab today and tomorrow. And after school I have to de-gum desks, so I'm also missing gymnastics practice."

"*Two days?* Oh, Maya, that's so unfair!"

"I know, right? But Hairy Hands told her I was 'challenging his authority.' I said, 'No, actually I was challenging *Chloe's* authority.' So he went, 'See? There she goes again! This has been the behavior pattern *all year*!'"

"Irk," I said.

"And then Fisher-Greenglass was like, 'Maya, you've disappointed me, I'm sorry if this punishment seems harsh, but you need to learn respect before you go off to high school. If this happens again . . .'"

Her forehead puckered. My best friend was super-competitive and superstrong, but she hated disappointing people. Especially people in charge.

"Well, it *can't* happen again, let's put it like that," Maya said. "My parents warned me that if I'm not on totally perfect behavior, they're pulling me out of gymnastics for the entire rest of the year. Can you believe that?"

"No, that's awful," I said. My first thought was: *Maya's parents are crazy. Glad* my *parents are so much saner!* My second thought was: *Yeah, but what if they take away my camera?*

"Oh, right," Maya added softly, "and while we're on the subject of me messing up, I'm really sorry about what I said to you at the end of Spanish."

"You said something to me? Huh, that's funny, because I didn't hear anything."

Maya's face relaxed a little. "Thanks, Finny." She touched my arm. "So anyhow. I guess you'll be taking care of Zachary the next two days."

"What?" I said. "Listen, Maya, I'm really . . . not so sure about that."

"Not sure about what?"

"The taking-care thing. And also Zachary."

Her eyes grew wide. "Seriously? Why?"

I almost mentioned the fist bump at dismissal yesterday, but I caught myself. Hearing how the Croakers were laughing at us would probably just upset her, and she already felt bad enough. Besides, I told myself, it wasn't Zachary's fault the Croakers were such jerks. Or even that they'd made him a Croaker hero, apparently.

And anyhow, it wasn't like the fist-bump thing was Zachary's only issue.

Instead, what I said was: "I don't know, Maya. There's just something funny about him."

"Really? You mean like funny weird?"

I nodded. "I can't put my finger on it. But doesn't it seem like he has certain expressions?"

"Oh, come on," she said, smiling. "Everyone has certain expressions."

"Yes, okay. But I mean, he says some things *a lot*. Have you noticed? All that stuff about second chances—"

"What's wrong with second chances?"

"Nothing! They're perfectly fine. But it's the way he keeps repeating it all the time. And it's not just that—he hasn't told us anything about what happened when he left Fulton, I'm positive he lied about writing 'lunch' on his wrist, and also—"

"Yes?"

I took a breath. "Well, don't you think it's slightly strange how he turned into a Frog? Without ever being a Croaker?"

Maya laughed. "You're still obsessed with that."

"Not obsessed. And I don't think he's an imposter. But—"

"But what, Nancy Drew? You think he time-traveled to the future? Or did a body-switching thing with someone? Or wait—I know. Maybe he's some sort of hologram!"

"Maya, stop it, I'm serious."

Sabrina Leftwich was walking toward us, making a *click-click* sound with her boots. We waited for her to open her locker, hang up her jacket, and take out a couple of textbooks. But she didn't leave. She just stood there, flipping pages, like she suddenly had this burning urge to read about the Continental Congress.

Maya murmured, "Careful, I bet you-know-who is spying for Chloe." Then she leaned in closer. "Oh, and on that topic, I obviously can't go to Chloe's party now. I mean after our big fight in Spanish."

"That's not so terrible," I said. "I mean, it's just Chloe's Stupid Party—"

"Yes, but the thing is, I invited Zachary to come with us."

"You did?" I stared at her. "When?"

"Yesterday. He called our house and my brother snuck me the phone." Maya poked me in the elbow. "He said *you* made him call me."

"I didn't force him. But yeah."

She was watching my face now. "Anyhow, he thanked me for sticking up for him. And he said he wanted to go."

"To Chloe's? *Why?*"

"Oh, come on, Finley. You remember how mean Chloe always was, how she used to kick him out. It was humiliating. And I think it's really, really important to him to feel like he actually belongs here now."

All at once I could see where this was going. "Listen, Maya," I began.

She did a pleading smile. "So *would* you go with him, Finley? So that he doesn't have to go alone?"

"Are you nuts?"

"Uh-*huh*." She laughed. "But what does that have to do with it?"

"Okay, I'm not going to Chloe's party with Zachary."

"Why not?"

"Because I'm not going if you aren't. I never wanted to go in the first place."

A bunch of sixth-grade kids began streaming toward our lockers. So I said as quietly as I could, "Maya, can I ask you something? Why do you care about Zachary so much anyway?"

Sabrina Leftwich slammed her locker door and spun her combination lock. When she *click-click*ed over to Dahlia Ringgold and Sophie Yang, two girls from the basketball team, I calculated that Sabrina had finally left the eavesdropping zone.

Then I just let it out. "Because I know he complimented your gymnastics, which was extremely Froggy of him. And of course there's the cuteness issue; I'm not saying it doesn't exist. But he's a *middle school boy*. And I thought you'd given up on that species."

Maya's cheeks splotched pink. "You think I'm that shallow—that I'd like somebody just because he complimented me?"

"No, no." I could feel my face getting hot. "But the way you're inviting him to everything—"

"Finley, I'm only doing that because *you* like him."

"What?" I said.

"You *like* him," she repeated. "I mean, don't you? You keep staring at him."

"That's because I don't trust him," I sputtered. "I've been trying to tell you that, Maya. That's my whole *point*."

She took my arm. "Look, Finley, don't be upset with me for saying this, but do you ever think you're possibly a little bit too hard on people? And maybe *that's* the reason you're having trouble with boys?"

"Excuse me?"

"I don't mean trouble; I take that back. I'm just saying, you know, all that Frog business, naming boys to categories based on whether their voices changed—"

"Are you serious?" I was gaping at her now. "The *Life Cycle* wasn't just about their dumb voices! It was about their *total behavior*. And, Maya, you did it too!"

"I know, it was both of us; you're right. But I'm thinking . . . maybe it's time to throw out the chart, okay? Because boys grow up; they all do. Eventually. Look at Zachary: Did you think he'd ever change? And he has. I mean, obviously."

She squinted. Then her face lit up, and she did her desert-island wave to someone behind my head.

Of course it was Zachary.

As soon as Zachary came loping over, I mumbled some excuse and fled the lockers. I just couldn't deal with him right then; my brain was in snow-globe mode. Partly it was because Maya had accused me of crushing on Zachary, but mostly it was this: Even though I'd gone to school that morning worried about my best friend, and feeling guilty (although all I'd done was try to rescue her from both Chloe and Señor Hansen), we'd gotten into a fight. And she'd called me boy-illiterate again. And made me feel like a baby for the whole *Life Cycle* thing, which she'd half invented.

Although, now that I focused on it, I couldn't think of the last time she'd updated the chart. Okay, but she still talked about doing upgrades, didn't she?

Except no matter how hard I tried, I couldn't remember the last time she'd decided a boy was Froggy, or had qualified for Croaker status. And I remembered something else—two days ago when I'd mentioned Wyeth Brockman's croak/blush/invitation, she'd acted like it didn't matter.

Really, the more I thought about it, the more it seemed that the *Life Cycle* had become my job lately.

All right, I told myself. So maybe it *was* my job.

But even if that was true, even if I'd become the official chart keeper, did that mean I was being "too hard on people"? Or that I "was having trouble with boys"?

I mentally scrolled through various boys on the *Life Cycle* chart. Just yesterday I'd upgraded Wyeth Brockman, so it wasn't as if I couldn't change my mind about people. When they deserved it.

And I could appreciate the niceness of complete Croakers—Drew Looper, to name one. For example, just last week we'd been laughing together in social studies about this Web comic we both liked called

Splat. Also, a few days ago he'd let me copy his math homework, and to say thanks I gave him half of my chocolate chip brownie.

See? Niceness. From both of us.

Oh, and also Ben Santino. After I'd decided he was too Croaker to crush on at Chloe's party, we had a really fun conversation about zombies. Which we both agreed were way cooler than vampires. Or werewolves.

So the fact that I'd listed Ben Santino as a Croaker didn't mean I couldn't see him as a person.

It just meant I couldn't imagine him as *date-worthy*.

Which was totally not the same as "having trouble with boys." Or "being too hard on people" in general.

As for staring at Zachary: All right, maybe I had been. But staring did not equal liking. I was a chart keeper, a photographer, a student of character. *Une stud-ent of charact-aire.* Staring was necessary, a part of the job. How could you notice things about people if you weren't focused? You couldn't.

At least, that's what I told myself in homeroom.

CHAPTER 11

Every June at Fulton Middle they had Student Recognition Day, but really, it should have been called Maya Lopez Day. For the past three years she'd won practically everything—prizes in math, Spanish, science, physical fitness, and character. Last year, she even won Perfect Attendance, which we always treated like a joke—ha ha, a prize for just showing up, how impressive.

What I'm saying is, I never thought very much about the fact that Maya was always around at school. She just was. Until that Wednesday (and Thursday), when she was banished to the computer lab, learning to respect Señor Hansen's authority. Maybe stop calling him "Mister," for starters.

And I suppose if we'd been able to walk to class together, and pass notes in social studies, like always, we could have talked it out, or I could have made a silly joke. Or something. Except now she was in computer lab jail. So how could I (a) explain that she'd hurt my feelings (again) but at the same time (b) get things back to normal between us? I couldn't imagine how to make these two opposite things happen, but all morning I couldn't think about anything else.

It didn't help matters that while Maya was imprisoned in the computer lab, I had to deal with the Official Gossip. Somehow overnight a rumor had gotten started that Fisher-Greenglass had suspended Maya for a full week, summoned her parents to school, and announced that Maya was forbidden to return to Señor Hansen's class until she had written a letter of apology in perfect Spanish.

In homeroom Sabrina asked me if it was true that Fisher-Greenglass was also making Maya write a letter of apology to Chloe, although in English. So I said that Maya didn't have to write any letters, not in pig latin or Esperanto or any other language, and furthermore, if Maya owed Chloe an apology, Chloe owed her one right back.

Then Sabrina said, "All right, well, I know Maya's your friend and everything, and you think she's so great, *but*."

"But what?" I said.

Sabrina pressed her lips into a straight line. "I don't know, Finley. Maybe you could think for yourself sometime?"

I couldn't believe that. I mean, this was being uttered *by Chloe's lapdog*.

Other people asked me if Maya was okay. They always tilted their heads to the side when they asked this, like one ear suddenly weighed ten pounds: "Is she okayyy?" Sophie Yang and Dahlia Ringgold even asked me in homeroom if I personally was *okayyy*.

"Why wouldn't I be?" I asked.

"Oh, because you guys had a fight," they explained sympathetically.

I almost asked which fight they meant—what Maya had said to me in Hansen's class yesterday, or what she'd said today at the lockers. But I realized it didn't matter. The Official Gossip version of our friendship was that we'd been arguing in public.

And for once, it was right.

• • •

With all of this going on, the last person I wanted to deal with was Zachary. I avoided him all morning, until fourth-period art.

For most of that class our teacher, Ms. Cronin, was describing the new project. She was a very sweet teacher, but she was a big explainer, always willing to re-explain things for the kids who weren't listening, then take questions from the kids who hadn't been listening to her re-explanation. Usually by the time we got to pick up our drawing pencils and actually do the project, the period was over.

I think most kids didn't care. But I cared, even though I'd always been a terrible artist. It was like I could *see* what I wanted to draw, but when I picked up the pencil, all I ever got was a stick figure, or a stick landscape, or a stick portrait. Everything looked boring and flat and generic. Even though I saw it as complicated and 3-D.

Anyhow.

That day Ms. Cronin was re-explaining about this sunflower painting by van Gogh. She said the thing about it was that it was specific. "Every one of these flowers has its own special, unique character," she declared, sweeping her hand over a big reproduction she'd glued to some poster board. "Doesn't it almost seem as if each flower in that vase should have its own name?"

"Yeah," Jarret called out. "I think the top one is called Kyle."

Kyle punched his arm.

"Ms. Cronin," Chloe said in her fake-sweet voice. "Didn't van Gogh do his painting in France?"

"Well, yes," Ms. Cronin said. "In Arles, which is in the south of France."

"I thought so. So shouldn't those sunflowers be named Jacques? Or Marie?"

Sabrina giggled. So did Olivia.

Ms. Cronin nodded patiently. "That's fine, Chloe. But let's forget about the names. All I meant was—"

She re-explained her point about how each flower, each petal, had its own special specialness. Finally she gave us our next assignment: Draw an object, any object, so that it seemed to have a "specific, unique character."

"Does it need to be a flower?" Cody Bannister asked.

"Not at all," Ms. Cronin said. "It could be a cat or a pencil or a quart of milk. The important thing is to really *see* it—"

Irk. More re-explanations.

If Maya had been there, we'd have been passing

notes about Cody's new haircut (too much mousse, or something; the front stuck out like a hood ornament). But she wasn't. And because by then I was crazed with boredom, I peeked over at Zachary.

He was talking to Dahlia Ringgold. Or rather, she was talking to him, saying something brilliant and enthusiastic like "Oh, I mean that's like so incredibly, omigosh, I don't believe it." When she finally stopped exclaiming things, Drew Looper reached over and shoved Zachary off his stool. It wasn't a mean shove; it was more a *way to go with the ladies* shove. Except he probably threw a "bro" in there also, because Drew Looper used words like "bro."

Way to go with the ladies, bro.

Snort. I mean, how excruciating.

And again, Zachary was grinning. Thereby proving, once and for all, that he didn't need me to "take care" of him. Despite what Maya had told me at the lockers.

Finally Ms. Cronin announced that in the remaining six minutes of class we should get started on our "sunflower-inspired" drawings, so I drew a bunch of daisies with berets and curly French mustaches. Only my drawing was so bad that I crumpled the paper into a ball and jump-shot it into the trash.

Suddenly Zachary was standing behind me. "Hey, two points," he said cheerily.

"You mean three," I said. "Here's the line." I tapped the chair behind me. It was a joke, but he just nodded like, *Oh right, of course I knew that was the three-point line.*

Then he cleared his throat. "Uh, Finley? Are you mad at me?"

"Why would I be?" I asked.

"I don't know. You were weird on the phone yesterday. You don't seem to be talking to me today. And this morning at Maya's locker, you took off as soon as I came over."

"Because I had to return a library book. To the library. Why do you think it was about you?"

"I just . . . never mind."

We stood there, not looking at each other.

"So I called Maya yesterday," he finally said. "She said Chloe was having this party on Saturday."

"Yup," I said.

"But Maya's not going. She said you were, though."

Great, great, great. "You know what, Zachary? Maya doesn't decide my calendar for me."

"Oh," Zachary said. "No, I know. That's not what I meant."

"Yo, Mattison!" Drew Looper shouted. "Someone is wai-ting for you."

Dahlia Ringgold swatted Drew's hand. "Shut up, you really, gah, I swear."

Then Jonathan Pressman pointed at Dahlia. "Hey, Mattison. Mattison, Dahlia just said—"

"One sec," Zachary called over his shoulder. His almost-purple eyes met mine. "Anyway, Finley, if I did something, I'm sorry." Then he went back to his table.

And I thought: *Sorry for what? Talking about me to Maya?*

Also: *Dahlia Ringgold? Please. She can barely form sentences.*

Also: *"Mattison"?*

I mean, okay: As a name it beat Freakazoid, but that was a pretty low standard. This seemed to me like a prime example of Croaker behavior: calling each other by their last names. What was wrong with using first names? Last names seemed so cold and imper-sonal. Generic.

Why did boys—specifically Croakers—want to be generic?

Why did Zachary?

CHAPTER 12

Three centuries later, school was over for the day, but I didn't wait on the steps for Maya. I figured she wouldn't show up, since she had to be degumming desks, plus I didn't want to deal with Hanna and Olivia. It wasn't just because I knew they would both want to talk about Maya. I also knew that Olivia would ask me to take her photo, and the truth was, I wasn't ready.

How can I explain this? Maybe it will sound crazy, but for some reason, ever since art, I couldn't stop thinking about those van Gogh sunflowers. They weren't the sort of perfect, supermodel bouquets you saw in flower shops or magazines. If you gave them to someone as a present, the person would probably say, "Hey, thanks for the half-dead flowers." But they were beautiful anyhow, because they were droopy. No—not because they were droopy. Because they looked real. The opposite of generic.

And I started thinking about all the pictures Dad took of me when I was little, how so many of them were from holidays and birthdays and vacations I couldn't remember. But if you asked me about all those events now, what I'd see was the photo. Really, it was almost as if the photo had replaced the memory in my brain.

So then I had this idea: Taking pictures wasn't just about showing my friends looking supermodel perfect. Some of these yearbook photos could actually be *what people remembered*. When they were ninety, someone could ask them if they remembered Olivia Moss from middle school, and they'd probably blank on the actual person. But maybe they'd see my photo of Olivia Moss. Or rather, their memory of my photo. And if my photo was just some zitless, fakey-fake fashion-mag pose, it would be like the actual, droopy-sunflower person named Olivia Moss never existed.

Same for Maya.

Also for Zachary, who I refused to photograph as generic "Mattison."

That is, if he still wanted me to shoot him for the yearbook. Which, come to think of it, I didn't know for sure, since it was Maya who'd told me he wanted a photo in the first place. And considering how I'd acted in art, it wouldn't be surprising if he changed his mind.

Anyhow, after basketball practice I decided to go home to read that book about portrait photography. Maybe I could learn something about taking ungeneric, sunflower-type portraits. Also, I desperately needed to clear my head.

The house was quiet when I walked in the door. Mom had left a note saying she'd taken the Terrible Two to Gymboree, so I made myself a mug of hot chocolate, brought it upstairs to my bedroom, and turned on my computer.

First I checked to see if Maya had e-mailed me. She hadn't, which was not a shocker, really, because you couldn't use the school computer lab for personal stuff. So I sent her a quick *hey, how did it go today* message to her home account, nothing about the *Life Cycle* or our sort-of-fight or Zachary.

Then, since my computer was on anyway, I speed-read Mom's blog to see if she'd written anything about

Awesome Daughter. This was what she'd posted today, around the time I was in art:

You all know how committed I've been to providing gender-neutral toys for the twins—unpainted blocks, puzzles, clay, etc. Gotta confess, guys, lately I've been wondering if maybe I should just give them the toys they clearly prefer—a truck for Max and a tutu for Addie.

If you give your toddler son a truck, will he end up hating poetry? If you give your toddler daughter a tutu, will she hate her body when she reaches puberty? Please tell me I don't need to worry about putting negative gender-typing thoughts into their impressionable little heads.

How gender-neutral is your toy box? Comment below!

Xox,

Jen

This was kind of warped, I thought. Most of my own toddler years were a swirly blur in my head, but I had a distinct memory of Mom handing me a Barbie on her way out the door to work. Did she actually believe that Dentist Barbie's voice chip had put "negative gender-typing thoughts" in my brain? Such as what—*brush your teeth every day*? And that because of Dentist Barbie I now "hated my body"?

Plus, it seemed she was saying that girls were as messed-up as boys when they "reached puberty." I was pretty much an expert on this topic, so really, if she wanted the truth about boys and girls, she should have asked for my input.

Well, she wanted comments, didn't she?

I typed:

Dear Mom,

You gave me Dentist Barbie when I was five and guess what—I don't hate my body. In fact, I currently practice good dental hygiene.

Love,

Awesome Daughter

And then, to prove that I was the Davis who knew about the Infinite Weirdness of Boys Reaching Puberty, I opened my science binder, took a sip of hot chocolate, and spent a few minutes updating the *Amphibian Life Cycle*:

<u>Drew Looper</u>: Croaker. Way to go with the ladies, bro. *shove*

<u>Jonathan Pressman</u>: Croaker. How long has he had that huge-ormous Adam's apple?? Looks like a wad of bubble gum stuck in his throat. Lately has developed a turpentine smell.

<u>Cody Bannister</u>: Tadpole with Croaker tendencies??? Wearing Angry Birds Band-Aid on left elbow. (No reason to assume it's ironic.) Bizarre new haircut, which possibly means he's attempting to give himself a Croaker makeover. Also said "Bless you" when I sneezed today in social studies, which for him is definite progress.

<u>Zachary Mattison</u>: Frog. Maybe too much of a Frog. Although now associating with Croakers and going by the Croaker name "Mattison." Can you be a Frog or a Frog-plus with Croaker tendencies? Can you evolve in reverse?

I stopped writing. The Mattison business reminded me of art, and I didn't want to think about that whole scene—Zachary apologizing, even though he didn't know what for, the way he'd mentioned Chloe's party, the nasty way I'd responded. Plus every time I thought about Zachary, it was like the *Life Cycle* got all muddled and muddy. How was I supposed to do meaningful upgrades, if everything Zachary did made me change my mind about him as an amphibian?

Okay, enough of this, I scolded myself. *I came straight home to study photography, not to obsess about stupid boys.*

I opened the *Amazing Face* camera book. For a long time I studied the portraits, especially the unbeautiful ones. Especially the eyes.

Then, on the empty pages that I'd been saving for more chart updates, I started taking notes.

The next morning I woke up feeling off balance. You know how when a wire gets broken in your braces, your whole mouth feels out of whack? Or when you lose your bracelet and it's like your whole body is tilted because there's nothing at the end of one arm?

That was me, because as soon as I opened my eyes, I remembered that yesterday I'd sort-of-fought with my best friend. Again.

The only thing to do was to get to school early. Maybe, I told myself, if I could spend five minutes with Maya at the lockers, we could unsay the things we'd said, and then things would be back to normal.

Except I never made it to the lockers, because that morning our house was utter chaos. Dad had left for an early meeting, and while Mom was trying to lure Addie to her potty, Max went zooming down the steps, crashing his knee into the banister. So then Mom went into EMT mode, trying to smear bacitracin on Max's knee even though he was thrashing around and howling about his "boo-boo." And of course *that* was when Addie decided that she needed to be on her potty NOW, but only if someone would sit with her and read *Princess Petunia and the Lost Tiara.*

In other words, me.

"Fin, honey, I don't know what I'd do without you," Mom said, as she was finally driving me to school. By the time Addie and Max had been calmed down, cleaned up, and strapped into their car seats, where they immediately fell asleep, I was about thirty minutes late. Although that morning I was only missing one of Fisher-Greenglass's assemblies about the Scary World of Online Identity Theft, so truthfully, since I'd already missed Maya, there was no big rush.

"Oh, Mom, I'm not *such* a help," I said. "Anyhow, *someone* had to read Addie's dumb book."

"Yes, of course," Mom said, smiling. "What I'm saying is, you give me hope that if I hang in there with Max and Addie, they'll turn out great. Just like you, Awesome Daughter."

My stomach knotted. Suddenly I remembered Awesome Daughter's comment about Dentist Barbie.

"Um, Mom?" I said. "By any chance have you checked your blog lately?"

"Why?"

"No big reason. I just . . . sort of posted a comment."

"On my blog? You did?" She glanced at me. "About what?"

"Nothing. Just that you gave me Dentist Barbie when I was little. And I turned out normal, right? Even though you didn't obsess about *my* toys."

Mom blew out some air. "Whoa," she said. "First of all, I *didn't* give you Dentist Barbie. That was a present from Grandma Annie. And actually, she wanted to give you Beauty Pageant Barbie or Bimbo Barbie, I can't remember which, but I told her absolutely not, I didn't want my young daughter to get unhealthy messages about her body, and we had a fight, so you ended up with Compromise Barbie."

"Oh," I said.

"Second of all, where did you get the idea that I *didn't* obsess about your toys? You mean because when you were little I had a full-time job?"

I shrugged. Really, it was just a feeling I had, but that didn't mean it was wrong.

"And third of all," Mom continued, "the next time you want to comment or discuss something—anything—just talk to me in person, okay? You're my kid; that blog is my job. Separation of church and state."

"Sorry," I mumbled. "I guess I was just having a bad day."

Mom shot me a look. "You were? You want to tell me about it?"

"Maybe later. But you can delete my comment, right?"

"Sure, of course." After a minute she said, "So. As long as you read my post, what did you think?"

"You really want to hear?"

"That's why I'm asking, Finley."

"Okay." I took a breath. "I think boys my age are a

completely different species, so it isn't fair to compare them to girls. Or to talk about "puberty" like it's all one thing. Because there's girl puberty and boy puberty, but the boy kind is definitely weirder."

"Oh," Mom said. "Is it."

I nodded. "Much. It's really obvious in a way, but also not. It's like, you look at a boy and you think, okay, he's growing up, he's losing his tail—"

"His tail?" Mom said.

"Not literally *his tail*. But then five minutes later the tail is back. Or he doesn't have a tail but now he's talking funny."

"You mean his voice is changing?"

"I mean he repeats himself, or he sounds like a cyborg. Or he starts referring to himself by his last name."

"Wow," Mom said. "That's very—"

"On the other hand, he's also apologizing, which is definitely Froggy. I mean, especially if he doesn't even know what he did wrong."

"*Did* this person do something wrong?"

"I'm not sure. But he's definitely hiding something, and maybe not just the wrist tattoo. As for toys," I said quickly, to change the subject, because maybe you shouldn't say "wrist tattoo" to your mom, "I don't think they matter as long as they aren't g-u-n-s." I spelled this in case M-a-x was listening in his sleep. "And I think the twins are fine, so you shouldn't worry."

"Ah yes," Mom said, smiling a little. "But worrying is my job."

"I thought your job was being this expert mom-person."

She laughed. "Wherever did you get that from?"

"Oh, come on, Mom. People listen to you. You have this blog and a podcast—"

"Finny, believe me, there are days when I feel like such an imposter."

"You?" I said.

"Let me tell you a big secret: There's no such thing as an expert mom. Expert moms do not exist in nature." She signaled as she pulled up to the front of school. "No parent has all the answers. We're all just figuring it out as we go along."

I don't know why I said this either, but I did: "Too bad you can't use mnemonics."

Mom kissed my cheek. "Yeah, well. Like you said, they don't work for everything. Some things you have to learn the hard way."

CHAPTER 13

That whole morning everything went wrong.

Since I'd missed Maya at the lockers, I tried two different times to get into the computer lab. But both times the door was locked, and when I tried at lunch, Señor Hansen was there with his seventh-grade class, which meant I couldn't exactly pop in for a quick visit. And because I definitely didn't feel like going to the lunchroom and dealing with day two of *Is Maya okayyy?*, I went to the library to hang out with Ms. Krieger. Except she was busy teaching the fifth grade about the joys of bibliographies.

So I went to the photography shelf, took a Diane

Arbus book, and plopped on the squishy red sofa.

For a few minutes I flipped the pages. Diane Arbus's photos were creepy, but I couldn't stop staring at them. You know the kind of dreams that aren't about you personally, but that you can't get out of your head all day? That's kind of how her pictures were making me feel—a little queasy, like I was reading someone's warped, private diary.

And finally I needed to get back to reality, so I opened my science binder to update the *Amphibian Life Cycle*.

Drew Looper: Total Croaker. Crashed into me with his backpack. Instead of saying "sorry" or "oops" merely grunted. Then blushed. Then asked if he could copy my math homework.

Kyle Parker: Croaker. Visible blob of zit cream on chin, looks like marshmallow fluff.

Finally I realized someone was standing in front of me. And that this person was Zachary.

"Hey," he said. "You weren't at lunch, and I remembered you liked hanging out in the library, so."

He handed me an unopened bag of mesquite-flavored potato chips.

Here is the thing: According to my taste buds, mesquite anything tasted like a mistake—smoky, burned, overspiced. And what a totally Croaker thing to do—present someone with a whole bag of awfulness without even knowing their taste buds' opinion on the subject.

On the other hand: Zachary had showed up with a food offering. Which was extremely Froggy of him, actually. Which no one had ever done for me in history, not even Maya. Plus, considering my nasty behavior in art yesterday, this was incredible.

So I took the bag.

"Ms. Krieger won't let us eat in the library," I said. "But thanks. I mean, a lot, Zachary."

"You're welcome." He did a pretend little cough. "Anyhow, um. So Sabrina says today's the deadline for yearbook photos. And I don't know if you still want to take my picture—"

"No, I mean, yes, I do."

"Awesome." He sat next to me on the sofa. "You're looking at photos?" he asked, glancing at the Arbus book.

"Yeah, I'm trying not to be an imposter."

"What?" He blinked.

"I mean, if I'm supposed to be taking pictures, I'd like to know what I'm doing."

"Cool," he said seriously. "I'm interested in learning about photography too. I think it's a great hobby."

Sometimes Zachary spoke as if he'd read a book called *How to Talk Like a Human Being*. But probably he should have read *How to Have a Conversation*, because when he said cyborg things like "I think it's a great hobby," I had absolutely *no* idea what to say back. Plus, he'd said almost this exact same sentence—"photography is a cool hobby"—the first time he'd called me on the phone. So this was another time when he repeated himself.

But (I argued with myself) despite the cyborg manners, Zachary was the first person who'd shown any interest in my so-called hobby. You couldn't count Ms. Krieger, because showing interest was her job. And really, all Maya and Olivia cared about was new yearbook photos.

Also, by then I was feeling depressed about the Maya situation, and I was desperate for some company. I figured I owed Zachary some niceness from yesterday. *Plus he'd brought me a food offering. Even though it was mesquite-flavored.*

So I said, "What about you?"

"Me?"

"What's *your* hobby?"

"Oh." He thought. "Dogs."

"You have one?"

"A mutt named Thor. My stepbrother Kieran has three. They're all rescues."

Okay, this was information. Except I didn't want to talk about Kieran or his rescue dogs. "So what else do you do?" I said, nodding the way you do when you want to keep someone talking.

"I don't know. I like drawing robots," he answered.

"Really?"

"What's wrong with robots?"

"Nothing. It's just . . . robots and dogs aren't hobbies."

"What are they?"

"Subjects."

Zachary shrugged. "Well, I disagree. Also I like graphic novels, but they're actually comics. And I like bad movies."

"You can't like them if they're bad," I protested. "That makes no sense."

"No, Finley, the badness is the whole point. But

151

they have to be terrible; I don't like them if they're mediocre. Mediocre is a waste of time."

I had to smile. These were all boy interests, and I didn't share any of them, especially not the bad-movies thing. But I liked what he'd said about mediocre. Mediocre was sort of the same as generic.

"Also you like basketball," I reminded him.

"I do?"

"Your hook shot?"

"Right. Yeah, I'm still working on that." He started tapping his foot. "So, um. The yearbook photo—"

"I haven't forgotten. Can I show you something first?" I flipped the pages of the Diane Arbus book.

"You *like* these?" Zachary said, looking over my shoulder.

"I wouldn't say *like*," I admitted. "But they aren't mediocre. I think they're incredibly . . . ugly-beautiful, like those sunflowers in art. And I guess I like *looking* at them."

"Why?"

"I don't know. They're good to think about." I pointed to a portrait of a massively tattooed bald guy. "Okay, so, if you look at this guy, doesn't it make you wonder what he ate for breakfast?"

"Not really," Zachary said. "I'm not sure he has teeth, actually."

"Sure he does. You can tell by the way he's scowling at the camera."

"Well, even if he does have teeth, I bet he doesn't eat breakfast. On principle." Zachary wrinkled his nose. "So what do you think Mr. Coffee has for breakfast? Besides coffee, I mean."

"Doughnuts," I said. "The really slippery kind."

"Boston cream."

"Spelled *crème*."

"Right," he said, smiling a little. "I bet Fisher-Greenglass has granola with soy milk."

"And Ms. Krieger has a croissant, or whatever she feels like. Maybe pizza or an ice cream sundae. What about Hairy Hands?"

"Blood oranges. Bloody steak. Or wait—what do they call it when steak is raw?"

"Salmonella," I said.

He was grinning now. "No, there's an actual French name for it. My stepmom watches all these cooking shows."

"Your stepmom?" I asked casually.

"Yeah, my dad's new wife. In Florida." His smile

twitched at the corners. "That's where I went last spring. My parents made me."

"Oh," I said.

"There was this whole big wedding thing, so." He shrugged. "But it turns out I have this cool step-brother."

"You mean Kieran, right?"

Zachary tugged on his sleeves. "Yeah. He's sixteen. He taught me a bunch of stuff, and he gave me some clothes when I outgrew mine."

Well, so that explained Zachary's style make-over, and the limited wardrobe options. It also explained why he'd acted so weird last year. And why he didn't exactly volunteer information when he came back. I mean, if my parents divorced and my dad moved across the country and got himself a new family they forced me to live with—well, let's just say I wouldn't be contributing that news item to the Official Gossip.

But now Zachary was being serious and quiet, and I wanted to get back to the fun we'd been having guessing our teachers' breakfasts.

"You know," I announced, "I strongly feel we should write down those menus. To commemorate them for all eternity." I grabbed my science binder and flipped to the back.

"What was that?" Zachary asked. He was peering over my shoulder.

"What was what?" I carefully wrote the words *Secret Breakfasts of the Fulton Faculty.*

"I don't know. You had a page that said something about tadpoles? And I think croaking . . . ?"

My heart crashed into my chest. I slammed the binder shut.

"Oh, that was nothing," I said. "We were studying frogs in science. Last fall."

"So why are there names?"

"Names?"

"Of kids. It looked like a list."

My brain emptied. "Those were just . . . to help me remember the material. I'm terrible in science, so I used a mnemonic."

"A what?"

"You know, a dumb memory trick. Like *i* before *e*, except after *c*. Or ROY G BIV. Or My Very Educated Mother."

"Every Good Boy Deserves Favor," Zachary said. "Thirty days hath September. HOMES."

"Exactly." I exhaled a little. "Homes?"

"*H-O-M-E-S*. First letter of each of the Great Lakes: Huron, Ontario, Michigan, Erie, Superior."

"Oh, right," I said. "Like PEMDAS in math—Parentheses, Exponents, Multiplication, Division, Addition, Subtraction. I can never remember the Order of Operations unless I write PEMDAS at the top of the page. Ha ha, isn't that pathetic?"

"I wouldn't call it that," Zachary said, shrugging. "I'm the same way."

Phew, I thought. I'd just saved this conversation from utter excruciation. But I still had to change the topic immediately. And permanently.

"Zachary?" I said. "Can I ask you something? You still want to go to Chloe's Stupid Party?"

He raised his eyebrows. "You mean with you?"

"Yeah. I don't mean *go with me*—"

"I know what you mean," he said. "And yeah. Actually, I do."

And then he gave me a smile so gorgeous and glowing and Froggy that all I could do was smile back.

CHAPTER 14

Before lunch was over, I snapped four shots of Zachary superfast.

The first and second ones were of him looking at the Diane Arbus book. He had a funny expression, like he was eating something that possibly tasted good, but he wasn't sure how he felt about the ingredients.

The third and fourth ones had him looking right at me. I mean, *at me*, not at the camera. Don't ask me to explain this, because I can't.

The photos didn't come out great. The library light was uneven, and Zachary was boringly centered in the composition. But it was amazing that the photos weren't blurry, considering how my hands were shaking the whole time.

Because Zachary Mattison had almost seen the *Life Cycle*.

Well, actually, no: He *had* seen it. He just hadn't known what it meant. And I'd managed to distract him with all those mnemonics, which maybe couldn't teach Spanish verbs or toddler raising but were good for some things, fortunately. Plus, of course, asking him to Chloe's Stupid Party—that was a good distraction too.

Which was why I did it, I told myself. *I mean, obviously.*

I also finally took Olivia's picture. It was at dismissal, and she didn't even know I was taking it, because I stood in the doorway and used the zoom while she was chatting on the steps with Hanna.

The strange thing was, until I looked at Olivia through the zoom lens, I never realized how much she fluttered her hands when she spoke. I wondered if she even knew that she fluttered her hands. Maybe when I showed her these pictures, she'd say, *Finley, that isn't me; that isn't what I look like at all.*

Maybe she thought of herself sucking in her cheeks like a supermodel. Or hideous with hidden zits. It was funny to think how people thought of themselves as much uglier than they were. Or more glamorous. The truth was, most people were somewhere in the middle. Besides, what you saw through the zoom wasn't the ugly/glamorous stuff, but the what-did-she-eat-for-breakfast stuff, the droopy ungeneric sunflower stuff. At least that was what I was looking for.

I took three photos, then watched Hanna run off to her mom's car and Olivia join Chloe and her entourage. Eighth grade was so predictable, I thought, like we'd all memorized a dance that we'd perform every day from now until the end of June. And we knew our steps so well we didn't need a mnemonic.

Even me, I admitted, as I started the walk home. That day the snow had thawed into a sort of slushie consistency, just wet enough to seep into your shoes and cold enough to freeze your toes. A school bus passed, spraying the snow slushie up on the sidewalk. And out of the open windows fifth-grade Tadpoles were screaming: *"You drink pus, you eat snot, you farted in the bathtub, smells like rot!"*

"Seriously?" I muttered. *I am sooo ready for high school.*

And all of a sudden I heard someone shouting: *"Fiiiiin, Finneeee, waaait."*

I spun around. Maya was racing toward me, her red scarf flying. When she caught up, we gave each other a long, swaying hug.

"Why aren't you degumming desks?" I asked, surprised. "Did you escape?"

She laughed. "No, I just told Fisher-Greenglass that I'd learned my lesson about respecting Mr.—I mean Señor—Hansen, and she took pity on me. Seriously, Fin, I was going mental in there. Where *were* you?"

I explained about the family chaos this morning, and how I'd tried visiting her twice, including at lunch. She crossed her arms while I was talking, like she didn't believe me, although possibly she was just cold. Then she asked me what she'd missed.

"Not much." I paused. "Oh, right. Actually, I'm going to Chloe's party with Zachary."

"WHAT?" Maya shouted.

"I asked him at lunch. Today."

"Omigosh. Finley. I *cannot believe* that."

"Don't shout," I complained. "Why can't you believe that?"

"Because you never do things like that. What happened?"

I told her about the library, leaving out how he'd almost seen the *Life Cycle* chart. The whole time I was talking, Maya was shaking her head in disbelief, like I was saying, *UNICORN! LOCH NESS MONSTER! I WON THE LOTTERY!*

It kind of annoyed me, to tell you the truth.

Jokingly, I said, "Hey, come on. It's not that crazy, okay?"

"Are you serious?" She laughed. "It's the Total Opposite of You."

By then we were in front of her house. We faced each other.

"What do you mean?" I said, not laughing. "The Total Opposite of Me?"

"Oh, you know. Relating to a boy as an actual person. Not just calling him an imposter hologram, or some kind of amphibian on that stupid chart. It's major progress; I'm really proud of you, Finley."

"*Proud* of me?"

"Is something wrong?" Maya asked, frowning.

I swallowed hard. It felt as if there were a grapefruit stuck in my throat. "You know what, Maya? If you don't want to do the *Life Cycle* anymore, if you think it's dumb or immature, or whatever, that's totally fine with me. Really. But please don't act like you never did it too, and please don't insult me about it either."

Her eyes grew wide. "How am I insulting you?"

"You're congratulating me for not being boy-illiterate anymore. Except I wasn't in the first place."

"Okay, that's really unfair," she said, taking a step back. "I never called you that, Finley, ever."

"No, Maya, you basically did." The words were tumbling out; I couldn't stop them. "I'm not saying I know everything about boy behavior, because I don't, and neither do you. Although I do know some things; I'm a student of character. So you shouldn't act superior all the time, like you are in charge of everyone."

"Oh," she said. Her mouth dropped open. "*Oh.* You think I act like that?"

"Sometimes yes," I said. "You can be. You keep deciding things for people without asking first. And yes, I still think there's plenty of weirdness about Zachary; I haven't made my mind up about him yet. But we talked, I know him a little better now, so I asked him about the stupid party. Although it's not a date, so please don't tease me about it, okay?"

"Fine," she snapped. "I won't even mention it. Can I say I'm happy for you?"

"Sure," I said. "I guess."

"Great. Then I'm happy! No, not happy—ecstatic!"

I watched my best friend stomp into her house and slam her door.

Mom put down her Wiggles mug as I walked into the kitchen. "You're late, Fin honey," she said. "Everything okay?"

"Oh sure, definitely," I replied, sounding not okay at all.

She got up from her laptop to hug me, and for a few seconds I rested my head on her shoulder. Mom smelled like a combination of talcum powder and the fresh-baked oatmeal cookies that were cooling on the counter. And maybe it was because of what had just happened with Maya, but the sweet, safe smells, plus the hug, plus the warmth of the oven, made me wish I could stay like that, in the kitchen, forever.

Finally Mom broke the silence. "Problem with Spanish?" she murmured into my hair.

"No, just the usual," I said.

"Boy weirdness?"

I blinked. "What?"

"This morning, in the car. You were talking about tails, boys losing tails, tails coming back—"

"Oh, right. Actually, today was more girl-weird."

"Was it," Mom said gently. She paused. "Everything good with Maya?"

That was when I broke out of the hug. "Why are you asking that? Who said anything about Maya?"

"Calm down, honey. You said 'girl-weird,' and she's your best friend, so—"

"Maya is fine," I said. "She's ecstatic. You want me to stay downstairs with Max and Addie? So you can work?"

Mom studied my face for a few seconds. Then she nodded. "Actually, thank you, Finny, that would be wonderful. I've got this podcast—"

"Hey, podcast away!"

I grabbed an oatmeal cookie and fled into the TV room, where the twins were sitting together on the sofa, sucking their thumbs and staring at Elmo. Without even thinking, I plopped beside them and opened my science binder to the back. Today there was plenty to update, but a lot of it was tricky—Ben Santino had held a door open in math (borderline Frog, except then he let the door slam); Trey Gunderson had done a burp-and-blush (Tadpole with Croaker tendencies? Hmm); Drew Looper had teased Dahlia about her new glasses (Croaker, but the humor was totally Tadpole). It almost seemed as if these boys were a messy jumble of ages—not simply one age, then graduation to the next age, in a neat, perfectly straight line.

Plus there was the library business with Zachary. The more I thought about our conversation today, the less sure I felt about how it belonged in the *Amphibian Life Cycle*. I mean, okay: the food offering was combination Croaker-Froggy, the awkward conversation parts were definitely Croaker, but calling robots a hobby was Tadpole; there couldn't be any different interpretation. And some of the other stuff I couldn't decide on. For example: Zachary used mnemonics—did I consider that Froggy only because I used mnemonics too? What about liking movies he knew were bad? (The bad-movie thing was Croaker, even Tadpole, but if you *knew* the movies were bad, did that make it Froggy?) Also, worshipping his teenage stepbrother— wasn't that Tadpole behavior, really? Croaker at the absolute most, but not Froggy. Definitely not Froggy.

Suddenly the whole *Life Cycle* seemed hopeless

to me. Hopeless and also utterly pointless. Because it seemed like everybody's cycles were speeding out of control. Overlapping with each other, and all of it turning into a blur.

Plus, without Maya, it wasn't even any fun. I hadn't wanted to admit this before, but it was true. Unfun and pointless, so why was I bothering? I couldn't come up with a single reason.

And it was strange to think this, but I thought it anyway: Maybe I'd outgrown the *Life Cycle* too.

I closed my binder, cuddled up to the twins, and watched *Sesame Street*.

That night I read this post on Mom's blog:

When you're the mommy of two-year-old twins, it's so hard sometimes to look up from all the chaos. Today I happened to look up and I noticed that Awesome Daughter had become a teenager.

This is exciting. It's also very scary, because I remember the drama of being thirteen. Will she be okay? Will she tell me if she isn't okay? How will I know things if she doesn't tell me? This morning in the car she began to open up—but the ride was short, and the conversation ended. Today when she came home from school she gave me a hug that was full of emotion—but shut down when I tried to probe.

With toddlers, you may not always understand what's in their little brains, but you're always able to clean up their messes (literally and figuratively). With a teen, you can't solve everything (heck, they won't even let you help drill Spanish verbs!)—but you can listen. Sometimes that's enough. So I'm hoping Awesome Daughter knows I'm available to listen, whenever she wants to talk.

Do you have similar experiences with your older kids? Any tips for encouraging communication? Comments below!

Xox,

Jen

CHAPTER 15

The first thing I did when I woke up that Friday morning was turn on my laptop to see if anyone had commented on the topic of How to Get Finley to Communicate with Mom. But the post was down. In its place was this:

Any feedback on Aunt Amy's All-Natural Bubble Bath? I tried some on Max and Addie during bath time, and I have to say, while I appreciated the chemical-free formula, I didn't love the bubble quality as much as . . .

Blahblahblah. It went on like this for seven paragraphs, and already there were five comments, plus Mom's responses.

This was definitely weird. I mean, not to brag or anything, but the post about me and how I wasn't communicating with Mom was a gazillion times more interesting. So I couldn't imagine why Mom had replaced it with this boringness about bubble bath. Maybe she'd gotten a lot of crazy-mom comments overnight.

Anyhow, it wasn't like I could ask her, because that morning she was having a late sleep-in. Dad made pancakes (apple cinnamon, which I could barely eat because I had zero appetite), we read to the Potty People (*Madeline* for Addie, *Green Eggs and Ham* for Max), and then, once Mom staggered into the kitchen, Dad drove me to school.

"Everything okay, Finster?" he asked casually, as we pulled up to the front door.

"Why wouldn't it be?" I snapped. "Why does everyone keep assuming I'm hiding information?"

"Maybe because you aren't sharing very much these days. Anyhow, we're here."

I sighed. "Yes, I know that Dad, and I'm really grateful. To you and Mom both."

"No," Dad said, smiling a little. "I mean, we're here *at school.*"

"Oh, right." I glanced out the window; a bunch of Croakers were shoving each other into a dirty snowbank. "Well, thanks for the ride."

"No problem. And you know, *we're here* the other way too." He winked, as if we were sharing a joke. "TGIF," he called as he drove off.

I took a deep breath and headed straight to Maya's locker. Not to apologize, I told myself, just to talk. About anything—the weather, Spanish verbs, the yearbook photo, which we still hadn't done.

But she wasn't there. Although for a second I wasn't even sure I was at the right locker, because for the first time in six weeks it was completely bare, all my birthday decorations—the orange and pink paper, the rainbow ribbons, the collage I'd made with photos of NYC, puppies, the Olympic rings, ice cream, fireworks—taken down, tossed into the recycling bin over by the exit.

The pancakes flipped inside my stomach.

I went straight to homeroom. Maya was sitting with Olivia; their hands were covering their mouths, which was kind of like putting a DO NOT DISTURB sign on their conversation.

Okay, I told myself. *They want privacy. I can handle privacy.*

But as soon as the bell rang, they both slipped out the door before I could catch up.

My heart banged as I walked into science. Maya and Olivia were talking to Mr. Coffee—or rather, Maya was doing the talking, Olivia was nodding, and Mr. Coffee was sipping his mug, caffeinating. I took my seat and watched him beckon to Sabrina, informing her she was switching lab stations with Maya.

"But how come?" Sabrina protested. "*Why* do I have to move my seat?"

"We're just making a few changes today," Mr. Coffee replied, as if that were a scientific answer.

So now Maya was deserting my lab station. She'd asked for a new seat because she didn't want to be best friends anymore. There was no other explanation.

My eyes burned as I took out my science binder, opened to a blank page, and wrote today's date.

"What's going on?" Zachary asked as he dumped his backpack on his chair.

"Not sure," I mumbled. Writing.

"I heard you and Maya had a big fight," Sabrina announced as she took Maya's seat. "Olivia told me."

Oh, fabulous, now we'd made the Official Gossip. "Whatever you heard, Sabrina, it's personal," I said. Still writing.

"Hey, don't get huffy with *me*. I think it's great you finally told off Maya."

"You did? About what?" Zachary demanded.

Holograms and amphibians. You. Although more than you. "Nothing," I said, flipping a page in my binder. "And can we please drop the subject? I'm kind of writing something here."

"You're always writing something." Sabrina smirked. "What's it now—an apology to Maya?"

"No."

"I bet it is. Can I read it?"

"No."

"Oh, come on, Finley. Pretty please?"

I didn't even answer that. I just kept writing: *Lalala, here I am sitting in science, ROY G BIV, PEMDAS, HOMES.*

And then: *ERRRRRRRRRRR.*

The sound vibrated through my bones. It made my hair hurt. We'd all heard that sound every few months for the last eight years, but even so, I'd never, ever get used to it.

172

"Fire drill, people," Mr. Coffee called out. "Leave all notebooks and backpacks at your lab stations, and proceed to the football field. You all know the drill. So to speak."

I stumbled down the steps and out of the building into the frosty air. In the corner of my eye I could see Maya huddling with a bunch of girls from our class, so I stayed on the other end of the field listening to Drew Looper brag to Zachary about how he beat some boring video game in one sitting.

Finally the end-of-drill bell rang, and before Maya could slip inside the building, I ran over to her.

"Can we please talk?" I said breathlessly.

Maya looked up at me. "What about?"

"Your seat in science."

"There's nothing really to talk about," she said. "I just think separate lab stations are better right now. For both of us." She bit her chapped lower lip. "And to be honest with you, Finley, I really can't deal with this right now."

"Okay, so when?" I asked, trying to keep my voice from squeaking. "When should we deal with this?"

"I'm not sure."

"We could meet here at lunch. I still need to take

your picture for the yearbook, remember?"

"Oh, riiiight," she said slowly. "You know what? Let's forget about the picture."

"Seriously? Because I know how much you hated that zit photo. Not that it was a *zit photo*."

She shrugged. "I don't even care about it anymore. Plus I'm pretty sure the yearbook deadline was today. And anyhow, it's not your problem."

My throat ached. Of everything she'd said to me up to that point, this hurt the most. Her problems were supposed to be my problems; if you looked up "best friendship" in the dictionary, that's what it would say. And I couldn't believe she didn't care about the zit photo. I mean, just a few days ago, the nose zit was all she talked about.

I blurted out: "Maya, listen, okay? I'm really sorry about yesterday."

"What are you sorry about?"

"Everything. That I hurt your feelings."

"But you're not taking back what you *said*." Before I could answer, she held up her hand like a crossing guard. "Look, I just think we need a little break from each other. I don't know, Finley. Doesn't it feel like lately all we do is argue?"

"Yeah, sort of," I admitted. "That's why I think if we could meet today at lunch—"

"We'd just keep fighting." Maya's eyes met mine. "Be honest. Wouldn't we?"

I wanted to shout, *we won't fight, I swear.* Except how can you argue that you won't argue? It made no sense.

By then we were the last people outside besides Mr. Coffee, and my eyes were beginning to sting. So I just mumbled, "All right, well, see you later," and went inside.

The instant I stepped back into science lab, I knew something had happened.

But it took me an extra two seconds to process these facts:

Mr. Coffee wasn't in the room.

People were crowded around my desk.

Sabrina was clutching my science binder.

Reading excerpts of the *Life Cycle.*

Out loud.

To the entire class.

"Wyeth Brockman: Tadpole with Croaker tendencies. Croaked on the word 'weekend.'

"Ryan Seederholm: Croaker. Smells like a gerbil.

"Jonathan Pressman: Croaker. His voice sounds like a chain saw shutting off in slow motion."

The words—my words—were pinballing around the room, randomly crashing into things, causing gasps and murmurs.

And laughs. From the girls, but not all the girls.

And none of the boys.

I wanted to shout, *Stop, that's private, give it back! Besides, it's not even what I think anymore. The* Life Cycle *is over!*

But I was frozen; I couldn't form words. I couldn't move, either.

And then Maya walked into the room. "What's going on?" she demanded.

"Finley's notebook," Chloe replied. "She's keeping some kind of warped rating system, apparently."

"Oh, really?" Maya said. "And if she is, why is that your business, Chloe?"

"Because it's *everybody's* business," Chloe answered. "I mean, if she just leaves it lying out on the desk. And if it's about all the boys in this room!"

Maya flashed me a panicked look. Then to Chloe she said: "Trust me, it's not a rating system."

"How do you know that?" Sabrina challenged.

Maya crossed her arms on her chest. "Because it's half mine. I half wrote it. And look, my name's even on the title: *The Amphibian Life Cycle (a.k.a. Finley & Maya's Super-Perfect Guide to Imperfect Boys)*. All right?"

The room went silent.

"Omigosh," Olivia exclaimed, her hands flying to her mouth.

At last I unfroze. "Actually, Maya just wrote one teeny little part, the bit about Dylan. I wrote all the rest. So if you guys want to be mad at someone—"

"We wrote it together," Maya interrupted. "As a team. I'm just as responsible as Finley."

Meanwhile, Sabrina was madly flipping pages. "Yeah, okay, so here's Maya's handwriting. 'Dylan McGraw: *ribbit!* Compliments Maya's knitting (scarf)! Saves M a seat in the lunchroom! Laughs at M's joke! Gorgeous smile!'"

Maya turned wild cherry.

Dylan put a book over his head.

Dahlia and Sophie went, "Aww."

"I think that's sweet," Micayla Hoffman said.

"Me too." Olivia grinned at Maya. "And not surprising. But I don't get the *ribbit* business."

"It just means Dylan's a Frog," I said quickly. "Which is like the highest form of praise. For a boy, I mean. It's complicated. Can I please have my notebook back now?"

"I don't think we're done with it yet, Finley," Chloe said. "And besides, what's so great about frogs? They're slimy and bumpy."

"And green," Sabrina added helpfully.

"Hey, I think frogs are cute," Olivia protested. "Remember Kermit?"

Sabrina snorted. "Olivia, you *would* remember Kermit."

It suddenly occurred to me that only the girls were talking. The boys were all staring at their shoelaces, at other people's shoelaces, at the patterns in the floor tiles. They didn't even seem angry; they just seemed embarrassed. Confused. Like they wished they could slip through a portal and come out in some alternate dimension. And right then, I wished I could join them.

But finally it was Jarret who spoke. "All right, this is stupid. And I don't get the point you're making—Frogs are cool, and Dylan's like the only one?"

"No, there are other Frogs," Maya said. She raised her chin at me. "Aren't there, Finley?"

I pretended to mentally scroll through a long list. "Um, sure. Let me think. Well, hmm, there's also Zachary."

Drew Looper shoved Zachary. *Way to go with the ladies, bro.* But this time Zachary wasn't smiling. And he wasn't looking at me, either.

"Though it's funny," Sabrina announced, pointing at my writing. "Because for Zachary it says, 'Total Frog. Apparently skipped (hopped?) over Croaker.' Whatever that's supposed to mean." She flipped a page. "But then here it says, 'Frog. Maybe too much of a Frog. Although now associating with Croakers and going by the Croaker name 'Mattison.' Can you be a Frog or a Frog-plus with Croaker tendencies? Can you evolve in reverse?'"

"That's not even English," Drew Looper grumbled.

"Oh, but we can figure it out," Chloe said loudly. "It's pretty insulting to Zachary, isn't it?"

Everyone stared at me then, even the boys.

"Look, it's not what I think anymore," I said. I could hear my voice wobble. It didn't even sound like my voice.

"Finley's changed her mind." Sabrina smirked

at Chloe. "She's a new person now. Since when—Monday?"

I peeked at Zachary. His mouth was tight, and his almost-purple eyes were fixed on me, trying to read behind my panicked expression into my brain. If he'd had a camera with him then, he could probably have taken an ungeneric portrait—*Girl Freaking When Her Thoughts About Boys—Specifically Zachary—Are Revealed to the Universe.*

And that was when Maya made her move. Like a tiny wild cat who'd been stalking an unsuspecting mouse, she suddenly pounced on Sabrina, snatching my science binder from Sabrina's hands. Really, it was a basketball move, a steal, and you could see by the look on Sabrina's face that she was shocked at losing possession to a puny gymnast.

"Here," Maya snapped, thrusting the binder at me. "Put that away! Or get rid of it!"

"I will," I said. "Thanks."

Maya shook her head, her ponytail swishing furiously. As Mr. Coffee sauntered through the door, she took her new seat on the total opposite side of the classroom.

CHAPTER 16

Sitting next to Zachary that period was torture. He kept avoiding my eyes and jiggling his leg the whole time, and once when I bumped his elbow semiaccidentally, he didn't even flinch or move or anything.

But then, about a minute later, he slid this note across our lab station:

So when I saw all that stuff in your notebook (when we were in the library) and you told me it was a newmonic (however you spell that word), you were LYING?

I wrote back: *Only because it was too complicated to explain!*

Zachary: *You mean too hard for my amphibian brain?*

Me: ☹ *Can we please talk about this?*

Zachary: *CROAK.*

That was it. He didn't write—or say—another word to me the whole rest of class. And as soon as science was over, instead of heading to English, I fled to the school library.

Ms. Krieger smiled as I crashed through the doors. "Some hot chocolate, *señorita*?"

She'd pronounced "chocolate" *cho-co-la-tay*. Like this was a pseudo-Spanish day.

I burst into tears.

Ms. Krieger sat me on her squishy red sofa. She handed me a mug, and a napkin, and said in a soft voice, "Talk to me, Finley. Fight with your best friend?"

I nodded. "And with everyone else. The whole class hates me now." I guess my hand was shaking, because she took the mug from me, and I wiped my nose with the napkin. "How did you know?"

"Oh, wild guess," Ms. Krieger replied. "And don't forget, I'm a student of character. Just like you."

"Better than me," I said, sniffling. "I'm terrible at it."

"Oh, I'm not so sure about that." She touched my shoulder. "What happened?"

I explained that I'd been "taking some notes about people," making it sound more *Harriet the Spy* than *Amphibian Life Cycle.* (Not to hide all the Croaker/Tadpole/Frog stuff, but because the last thing I wanted to do was explain all those standards to a teacher, and anyhow the specifics weren't the point.) And I described how Chloe and Sabrina had humiliated me, reading my words out loud in a way that made me seem boy-hating. Snarky. Even though I'd taken all those notes as a kind of science project. As a public service, almost. As a way of dealing with boy immaturity. Which, as all girls knew, was a major issue.

Ms. Krieger just listened. Finally she said, "You know, this sort of thing happens in the eighth grade every year."

"It does?" I said. "Someone steals a notebook—"

"No, I don't mean this exact situation. I mean there's always some sort of end-of-the-year kerfuffle." I must have stared at her blankly, because she said, "You don't know that word?"

I shook my head.

"Ah. So if we don't know something, what should we do then, Finley?"

I rolled my eyes. "Look it up."

Sometimes I forgot that Ms. Krieger was a librarian.

She walked over to the big gold dictionary she kept on a stand beside her desk. I watched her flip the pages. "'Keratin,' 'kerchief' . . . ah, there it is: 'ker-fuffle.' 'Informal, chiefly British. From Scottish Gaelic *car*, meaning twist, and *fuffle*, to disarrange.' The first definition is 'commotion, disorder, agitation.' More colloquially, 'hoo-hah,' 'hurly-burly'—"

"I think I get it," I said, sighing. "You're saying eighth graders are completely predictable, and that's why there's always a big fight this time of year."

"Well, yes, I suppose I am." She looked at me over her lime-green glasses. "My theory is this happens because you're graduating soon. And that's scary, so you pick fights. To distract yourselves."

"Actually, I think we pick fights because we're totally sick of each other."

"It may seem that way now." She smiled. "But believe it or not, some of the people you like the least in middle school may end up being your buddies in high school. I can't tell you how often I've seen that happen."

I'd stopped shaking by then, so she gave me back the mug of hot chocolate. And I was grateful to have it, because I had nothing to say to that last speech of hers. Buddies with Jarret and Chloe? Or with Sabrina? Because okay, I knew people changed, but there were limits.

I mean, there had to be. Even in high school.

Ms. Krieger closed the dictionary. "Anyhow, Finley, I was thinking. I desperately need to restore order to nonfiction, especially US history, which the seventh grade turned into mush after their last research assignment. If you have any time, I could really use your help."

"Me?" I asked. "You mean now?"

She nodded. "It's a big job, so I'll need to write your teachers a note. But I'm sure they'll allow it, because they're all deathly afraid of me. Okay with you?"

Was she serious? It was better than okay. "Thank you, Ms. Krieger. For everything."

"*De nada,*" she replied. "Now finish your cho-co-la-tay, *señorita,* and then *vámonos.*"

She wasn't exaggerating; the seventh grade had rear-ranged practically the whole nonfiction section. It took me the rest of the morning to hunt down the books and then get them returned to their right shelves. But when I finished, Ms. Krieger said I could hang out in the library, because, *quién sabe*, she might discover another kerfuffle on the shelves. That was the word she used: "kerfuffle," even though it was a pseudo-Spanish day. So I stayed.

At dismissal I slipped outside through the cafeteria door. Maya was standing in our usual spot, and I knew it would be weird if I just showed up and acted all normal like, *Hey, Maya, and how was your day*? And I didn't want to deal with Sabrina, or with Sophie and Dahlia, for that matter, so I skipped basketball practice too.

The strange thing was, I found myself taking the long way home, on Zachary's street. What was I thinking? Maybe if we ran into each other I could explain? (Explain what, exactly? I didn't even know: *Yes, I wrote that stuff about you, but accidentally/as a joke/my pen was taken over by mind-control zombies?*) But still I walked down Spruce Street, passing the squirrels and the hydrants and the little kids, whose messes were the kind their mommies could clean up for them, literally and figuratively.

And in front of a rusty mailbox on the corner of

Cypress I almost crashed into Wyeth Brockman, who was putting out his recycling.

"Hey, Finley," he said. "More surveillance?"

"What?" I nearly screamed.

"I meant of the block," he answered. "Remember? You were taking photos? For *The Bug*?"

"Oh, right. No, I'm done with all that. I was just walking. Just to . . . walk."

He picked up a milk container that had blown out of the recycling bin, and carefully squeezed it in with empty containers of cat litter, detergent, orange juice. All the stuff that made up a week of life in the Brockman family, I guessed. If I'd had my camera, I'd probably have taken a picture. And it would be a portrait, even though it had no people.

Wyeth watched me study his garbage. "School sucked for you today, didn't it," he said.

"Yeah, that basically sums it up."

"Well, you shouldn't feel so bad," Wyeth said. "Chloe and Sabrina had no right to read your notebook. And hey, they should talk—they've called people worse things than Tadpole. Remember Freakazoid?"

I kept nodding. Of course I remembered Freakazoid.

And then I saw something in Wyeth's pale blue eyes, a flicker I probably should have noticed before now. Maybe I should just shut up, I told myself. Or maybe not.

"They picked on you, too?" I asked him.

"Yeah," he answered, shoving his hands in the pockets of his hoodie. "Since practically the first day of middle school. But mostly they acted like I wasn't there, like I was a negative number or something. And you never did, or Maya, either. So if you wrote that my voice was changing—"

"Which is not a *bad* thing," I cut in. "By the way."

He shrugged. "Whatever. It's not bad or good; it's just true—my voice *is* changing. It's supposed to, right? Anyhow, what I'm saying is, I don't care about your notebook."

"Thanks," I said. "But I'm pretty sure other people do."

The weather was chilly and raw, and I felt exhausted from this long day, but I thought how sweet Wyeth was to be talking to me like this.

Because really: I'd made fun of his Tadpole-ness, hadn't I? We'd never intended the *Life Cycle* to be mean, but it kind of was, the more I thought about it. And now, despite everything I'd written, everything the class had heard, here was Wyeth acting Froggy.

If I'd still been keeping the *Life Cycle*, Wyeth would definitely have deserved an upgrade. Seriously, I would have switched his status to Frog right there.

But I wasn't the official chart keeper anymore. Nobody was. Anyway, the *Life Cycle* was over.

It occurred to me then that Wyeth's house had a basketball hoop in the driveway. "Hey, Wyeth, you want to play?" I said, pointing to the basket.

"You mean, now?" He looked confused. "You against me?"

"Why not?"

"I don't know. Because you're a girl?"

"No duh," I said, grinning.

"And you're on the team."

"Playing bench, but yeah."

"And you're much taller than me."

"True. You scared I'll shame you?"

"No." He laughed.

"Get your basketball, then," I challenged him. "One-on-one. But I'm not going easy on you, Wyeth."

"Yeah, Finley, I'm not going easy on you, either," Wyeth replied.

For about a half hour we played in his driveway. It was fun, even though we didn't bother to keep score.

Although if we had, I'm positive I would have won.

By the time I walked into the kitchen, Mom had morphed into Detective Mom. Señor Hansen had e-mailed her to say I was "illegally absent" from his class, so she'd called Ms. Fisher-Greenglass's office to sort it out. Somehow Ms. Fisher-Greenglass had heard I'd spent the afternoon in the library, so Mom called Ms. Krieger, who used the word "kerfuffle" and said I'd seemed "a tad upset." So Mom thought, *Oh, poor Finley, she's having a rough day; I'll pick her up from basketball practice and take her out for a cupcake.* But when she got to the gym with the Terribles, who were collaborating on a tantrum, Coach Malecki told her I'd never showed up for practice. Mom started to freak— she tried calling my cell, but Ms. Krieger had made me turn it off when I was in the library, and I'd forgotten to turn it back on. So then, from the parking lot, Mom called Maya's mom, who told her the whole story.

Well, not the *whole* story—Mrs. Lopez had heard from Maya about my notebook being read aloud, and how Maya had defended me, even though I'd insulted

Maya the day before. Maya hadn't told her mom about the *Life Cycle*, specifically—but she'd been updating her mom about what a good, loyal friend she was and what a bad friend I was being lately.

"Of course, I don't believe any of that," Mom added immediately. "But, honey, if you just skip basketball practice, and you don't keep me in the loop—"

"Mom, I'm sorry," I said. "I'm not deliberately hiding things. It's just I know how much you have going on."

"*You're* what I have going on," she said. "Nothing is more important to me than my Awesome Daughter. Don't you know that, Finley?"

I opened my mouth to say something. Not that I had a plan for what that would be—probably some mash-up of *I was just shooting hoops with Wyeth Brockman/sorry I made you worry/I'm mad you talked about me to Maya's mom/this was a terrible day and please don't make it worse by guilting me out/I love you too/can I please switch schools after the weekend?*

But what I ended up saying was this: "How come you took down that post?"

"What post?" Mom asked.

"You know. About getting me to communicate."

Mom smiled a little. "Because I realized it was a message to you. Not the business of the entire blogosphere."

And then Addie ran into the kitchen wailing because Max had tossed her stuffed pig into the toilet. So we spent the next twenty minutes giving Oinky a bubble bath and a blow-dry, while Max snuck into the upstairs bathroom and calmly ate an entire cherry ChapStick.

Once when I was in elementary school, Maya's mom took Maya and me to see some Chinese acrobats. I don't remember very much about the show, but I do remember one act they did. The way it worked was this guy lined up a bunch of poles onstage, and at the top of each pole was a plate or a bowl he had to keep spinning, no matter what. If a plate started to wobble, he'd run over to the pole and jiggle it just enough to keep the plate spinning.

Sometimes this was how it felt to be in a family with the Terrible Two. Especially on Saturday afternoon, which was when Mom drove off to do her errands, go shopping, have coffee with her friends, leaving Dad and me in charge. And I know Mom did it on her own every other day of the week, but on Saturdays it took both of us—Dad and me—to keep the plates from smashing to the floor. Every time Max had a potty accident, or fell and bumped his head on the coffee table, Addie would be finger-painting ketchup on the refrigerator door, or dialing numbers on the kitchen phone, or "typing stories" on Mom's laptop. I mean, seriously, the house was a loony bin.

The good part was that I didn't have time to obsess about the *Life Cycle*, or my ex–best friendship, or the fact that I'd invited Zachary to Chloe's Stupid Party, which would be taking place that very evening. Maybe if I'd had a few quiet seconds to think, I'd have wondered if I needed to call Zachary—or if it was totally obvious to him that I didn't exactly feel like hanging in Chloe's basement with most of our class and specifically *with him*, considering he probably detested me for eternity for what I'd written. And for the way it was broadcast to the class. And for lying about the mnemonics.

But all that Saturday, I was crazy-busy helping with the Terribles. So I didn't call him.

And he didn't call me.

Which made me think the word "croak" was

the last thing he'd ever say to me. No, write to me; I couldn't even remember our last real conversation.

Around five o'clock Mom finally showed up with six bags of groceries.

"So what's the state of your room?" she asked me.

"My room? I haven't noticed," I said.

"Go notice," she commanded, unpacking marshmallows, presumably for some Max-and-Addie art project.

I couldn't imagine why she suddenly cared about my room. But by then I was wiped out, so I gladly flopped on my bed, not caring that it was messy, or that the state of my room—exactly like my life—was a disaster.

And maybe two minutes later I heard the singing.

CHAPTER 17

We're the Green Girls
Loyal and true,
Happy together
Never blue . . .

Hanna and Olivia were standing on my doorstep, belting the Green Girls theme song—or anyway, one of them—at the top of their lungs. They were carrying backpacks and what looked suspiciously like sleeping bags.

"Um, hi?" I said, confused.

"We're serenading you," Hanna explained, laughing.

"Thanks," I said, because you don't get a serenade every day. "It's very . . . tuneful. Shouldn't you guys be getting ready for Chloe's party?"

"We're not going," Olivia said. "We're having a Green Girls reunion instead."

I stared. "You mean right now? *Here?*"

Olivia grinned. "Well, not on your doorstep, Finley; it's a bit chilly for that. But if you invite us inside—"

"Oh, sure. I mean, sorry." I led them into the front hall, my brain skittering to catch up. "Please excuse the floor; it's full of Smiley-O's. Oh, and squashed Play-Clay bits. Sorry. There are all these *toddlers* in this house—"

"Stop apologizing," Hanna said. "I wish I had cute little babies at my house. All I have is a grumpy big brother who leaves his socks in the bathroom."

"And *my* baby sister turned eight; can you believe that? Now she steals my nail polish," Olivia added. Her eyes traveled down the hall to the kitchen. "Whoa, you know what I just realized? I haven't been over since we stopped having troop meetings here."

"Me neither," Hanna said delicately. "That feels like centuries ago, doesn't it?" She paused. "I was really happy when your mom called, Finley."

"She did?" I said. "When?"

"This morning. She said it was supposed to be a surprise."

A surprise for me. Huh.

At that precise moment Mom walked downstairs, carrying Addie. "Well, hello there, girls," she called out in her troop-leader voice. "Long time no see."

"Hi, dirls," Addie echoed, waving her hand like Princess Kate.

Hanna giggled and waved back. And Olivia squealed, "Ooh, is this Addie? She's adorable."

"A doorbell," Addie agreed.

"Not *a doorbell*; *adorable*," I corrected my sister. "A-dor-a-ble."

"NO, NO, FIN-NEE," Addie shouted. "A DOORBELL." She gestured toward the front door with her entire body.

Because sure enough, someone was ringing the bell.

"Who can that be?" Mom asked brightly. "Why don't you answer it, Fin, honey?"

But she didn't wait to see who it was; she just herded Addie, Hanna, and Olivia into the kitchen. My stomach twisted as I turned the knob. Judging by Mom's ultra-convincing reaction, I knew it probably was Maya.

And two points for me, because it was.

"Hey, hi," she said softly. The tip of her nose was red from the cold; it matched her scarf, which she'd wound twice around her neck.

"Hi," I said.

"You disappeared yesterday after science. I was worried about you."

"You were? I just went to the library. Ms. Krieger let me hang out. But I'm fine now."

"Well, that's great. You're so lucky she likes you."

"Yeah, I know," I said.

Neither of us spoke.

"Okay if I come in?" Maya asked, tugging at her scarf.

"Oh. Sure, of course." I did a stupid *voilà* gesture. "Hanna and O are here too. It's like a surprise party. Except it's not my birthday. Which I'm sure you know." I could hear myself babbling, but I couldn't help it. "Apparently, Mom put together this Green Girls reunion thingy. Behind my back."

"Don't be mad at her, Fin. She just thought you needed your old troop mates," Maya murmured. "But I'll leave if you want."

"Why would I want that?"

"I don't know. Because we're having a fight? And you're mad at me?"

"Maya, *you're* the one who's mad at *me*."

She let out a long, noisy breath, a combination sigh and groan. "Yeah, well," she said. "I *am* still mad about the *Life Cycle*, which I *cannot* believe you left on your desk."

"Me neither," I admitted. "It was dumb. Even though Mr. Coffee said to leave our stuff."

"Uh-*huh*." Maya chewed her lip. Then she said, "But I'm *really* mad at Chloe and Sabrina. They were utterly despicable, the way they kidnapped your notebook. And reading it out loud was just *mean*."

"It was, wasn't it?" I said eagerly. "Not just to us. Also to the boys."

"I totally agree. Also, I've been thinking about the stuff you said, how I've been acting superior and all that."

It was my turn to groan. "Maya, can we please forget what I said?"

"No, because you were right; I get impatient sometimes, so I try to push things along when I should shut up. Oh, and on the topic of not shutting up: What I said about you and boys—"

"Maya, really, you don't have to—"

"The thing is, I wasn't *trying* to be obnoxious."

"I know."

"But it kept coming out wrong, and I couldn't make it right. Anyhow, I know I screwed up, and I'm sorry."

"It's okay," I said. Then I corrected myself. "I mean, I forgive you."

She threw her arms around me. It was always awkward hugging Maya, not just because of the height difference between us but because she hugged so tight it made me lose my breath.

But we were back to being friends. That was the main thing. And despite Maya's hug, which squeezed all the oxygen out of my lungs, I felt like I could breathe again, for practically the first time all week.

Finally she pulled away and grinned at me. "Hey, Fin, I just thought of something. If this is a Green Girls reunion, that means we're having s'mores, right?"

I was about to admit that I didn't know. But suddenly I remembered Mom unpacking the marshmallows. They weren't for some toddler art project; they were for us, obviously. My mom was the Best Former Troop Leader Ever.

"Actually, I'm just about positive we are," I told Maya, as the two of us ran into the kitchen.

That night was ridiculously fun. It wasn't just the s'mores and the pizza Dad made for us from scratch—we watched *Letters to Juliet,* our favorite movie from a zillion years ago. Hanna said she thought she had it memorized, so to test her we turned off the sound. And then the four of us started saying the mushy-romantic lines in Muppet voices, making each other laugh so hard I ended up with a stomachache and hiccups.

But the best part was what *didn't* happen that evening: no talk about Chloe's party, or the *Life Cycle,* or Zachary, or boys (in particular or in general). I wondered if Mom had told them that this was the rule, or if Maya had, or if all four of us just figured it out on our own. Anyhow, it happened; I was grateful—and almost felt like I was back in elementary school, when everything was unweird and unmessy and uncomplicated.

At ten o'clock Mom told us it was time to head upstairs and roll out the sleeping bags. (She knew us too well to expect us to go to sleep—I could tell she just wanted us in my bedroom so that *she* could go to sleep. But I didn't argue.) Anyhow, I'd decided it wouldn't be fair if I was the only one to get a bed, so I took my old sleeping bag down from my closet, unrolled it, and breathed its familiar, slightly sour-cheese smell. Then I grabbed my pillow and settled on the rug next to Hanna.

"Hey, Fin," Hanna said, giggling. "Remember that time in third grade we vowed to stay up until midnight? And you and I were the only ones who made it?"

"Yeah." I laughed. "I'm not sure what we thought would happen. Balloons, confetti . . ."

Suddenly I could hear my ringtone across the bedroom. It was coming from the front pocket of my backpack.

"Hey guys, what time is it?" I asked, unzipping my sleeping bag to check the alarm clock next to my bed: 10:13. Who could be calling me so late? Probably a wrong number.

"Gah," Maya said, annoyed. "Finley, would you hurry and answer that thing."

"Sorry." I dug into the front pocket of my back-pack and grabbed my cell. And my heart skittered when I read the caller ID: MATTISON.

"Hello?" I said.

Silence.

Then this: "Grrrk."

"Hello?" I said again. "Zachary? I think we have a bad connection. Can you hear me?"

"GRRRRRRGGGGGKKKK." It sounded like someone burping into a fist, followed by muffled laughing. Two different pitches. Maybe more than two.

And then this: "Rrrribbit. Rrrrrribbit."

My face burned. I hit End.

"Who was that?" Hanna asked, frowning.

I shook my head. I couldn't talk.

"Finley?" Maya said. She was sitting up in her sleeping bag. "What *exactly* just happened?"

"Prank call," I finally replied. "Or should I say, *croak call*."

"What?"

"I think it was Zachary and some other boys, teasing me about the *Life Cycle*. They were making noises—"

"Noises?" Olivia said. "Like what?"

"You know. Frog noises. Ribbit, ribbit."

"Oh, I get it, it's because of that list thingy you guys wrote," Hanna said. "What was it called again?"

"*The Amphibian Life Cycle*," I said miserably. "You heard about it?"

Hanna nodded. "From Sophie Yang. But the whole grade's talking about it, actually. I know it's a sensitive subject—"

"Uh-*huh*," Maya said.

"—but it's based on boy immaturity?"

Maya and I exchanged glances.

"Yeah, basically," I said. "But not just physical. It was more about their behavior."

"Also their manners, right?" Hanna said eagerly. "Which I totally think is a huge big deal."

"Maybe. Maybe not. I guess it depends." I sighed. "You know, I don't understand how Zachary even got my cell number."

Maya started zipping and unzipping her sleeping bag.

"And anyhow," I said slowly. "I really meant it when I told people that I'm done with the *Life Cycle*. And so is Maya."

"I was done with it first," Maya said. "Technically."

"Oh, but why, you guys? It's genius," Hanna exclaimed.

I rolled my eyes. "Okay, thanks, but that's slightly—"

"No, no, it's true; everyone loves it," Olivia interrupted. "Well, okay, not *everyone*. Not the boys, obviously.

And not Chloe and Sabrina. But yesterday, after science, all the other girls in our class were calling it brilliant."

"They were?" I said, shocked. "Like who?"

Olivia started counting on her fingers. "Sophie, Dahlia, Micayla—"

Maya's cell rang. Our eyes met.

"Answer it," I told Maya. "But just hang up if it's them, okay? Don't talk!"

She jumped up to get the cell from her jeans, which she'd draped over my desk chair. "He*llo*?" she said in a warning voice.

Hanna, Olivia and I crowded around Maya. We could hear croaking. A chorus of pseudofrog music.

"Ha ha, hilarious," Maya snapped. "Do you think we don't know who this is?"

"Hang up," I hissed.

She ignored me. "All you're doing is proving our point, that you're all hopelessly immature. Go ahead, keep making jerk noises. I can't *believe* you'll be graduating from middle school in a few months. *It's such a joke*."

Maya flung her cell on my bed.

"Gah," she said. "How humiliating."

"They only humiliated themselves," Hanna said soothingly, patting Maya's back. "It's like what bratty little kids do in third grade. Although funny that that was Zachary. I mean, he doesn't seem like the prank-caller type."

"Um, I'm not supersure about that," I said slowly.

"What do you mean?" Hanna asked.

"Finley knows Zachary better than anyone," Maya announced. She jutted her chin at me, as if she thought I'd argue that point. "It's true, Fin. You do."

And I had to admit that maybe I did, but that was only because everyone else had decided he was Freakazoid. And then Cute Boy. And then didn't bother to get to know the real person.

"Listen," I said. "I'm not saying Zachary is un-nice, or anything. Just that I think he's sort of complicated, so I wouldn't assume there's stuff he *wouldn't* do. And right now he's definitely mad at me, so there's that." I took a breath. "Plus the calls were from *his phone*—the caller ID said Mattison."

"That doesn't prove it came from *him*," Hanna argued. "Zachary was at Chloe's house tonight, wasn't he? Someone at the party could have been using his phone. And that would explain how he got Finley's cell number."

"True," Maya said. "For all we know, it could have been Chloe and Sabrina."

"No way," Olivia said. "Chloe would never do something like that."

Maya raised her eyebrows. "In other words, Olivia, you're sticking up for Chloe. Because you guys are such tight friends, right?"

"Hey, I'm not sticking up for anybody," Olivia answered. "And frankly, I'm not even sure I *want* to be Chloe's friend anymore. Or Sabrina's, either."

"Seriously?" Maya said.

"Not after what they did with Finley's notebook. Not to mention the whole party business."

"What whole party business?" I asked.

Olivia fluttered her hands through her hair.

"Tell us," Maya said. "Olivia, *what* whole party business?"

"Fine," Olivia blurted. "I was the one who invited you guys to Chloe's. Not Chloe."

Maya punched the air. "Ha, I *knew* it! Didn't I, Finley? Didn't I say *exactly* that thing, that I didn't believe Chloe's so-called invitation?"

"Yeah, you did," I said impatiently. "But let's forget about the Stupid Party, okay, you guys? About the *calls*—"

"Which Chloe would never do," Olivia said flatly.

"She'd totally think prank calls were babyish."

Hanna nodded. "I agree. Chloe's big thing is acting all cool and sophisticated. I can't imagine her making frog noises."

"Mayyybe," Maya said. "I personally think that girl is capable of anything."

"Can we please stay on topic?" I begged. "All we know for sure is that the calls were made on Zachary's phone during Chloe's party, and that it was at least two people."

Maya poked my ribs. "Woo, Nancy Drew."

I poked hers back.

"All right, but that still doesn't prove it was Zachary," Hanna insisted.

Maya crossed her arms. "Hanna, it sounds like you're trying to prove he's innocent. Don't tell me you *like* him."

"Of course not," Hanna replied. But she was blushing hard. "I just think we need more facts before we accuse anyone. A lot of things could have happened. Maybe a bunch of idiot boys borrowed Zachary's phone while he was dancing, or something."

I didn't know which was worse—Zachary prank-calling my cell with a bunch of Croakers, or Zachary going to Chloe's party without me and dancing, presumably *with* someone. Both of those images were unthinkable, so un-Zachary.

But who was Zachary, anyway? As I rezipped myself into my smelly sleeping bag, I mentally scrolled through all the Zacharys I knew:

Uber-Tadpole.

Freakazoid.

Frog.

Frog-plus.

Possibly Prince.

Liar (about the wrist tattoo).

Cyborg-mannered conversationalist.

Repeater.

Hook-shotter.

Frog with Croaker tendencies.

Croaker hero.

Nice boy in library.

Stepbrother in borrowed clothes.

Prank caller.

Crush. (All right, mine. For a little while. But in the past tense, the imperfect, because it happened for like a day and a half. Maya's too, obviously, also in the imperfect. And Hanna's, but in the present tense. Probably Dahlia's. Other girls too, I bet.)

And this wasn't even a complete list. Maybe there were other Zacharys I hadn't even met yet. Maybe the more time I'd spend with this person, the less I'd know who he really was.

If I'd even spend more time with Zachary.

If I even wanted to.

CHAPTER 18

To be honest, I was dreading breakfast the next morning, because I had a feeling the four of us would still be arguing about the calls. But what I forgot was the Davis Chaos factor, the way Sunday breakfasts at our house were plate-spinning extravaganzas, with the Terribles zooming around the kitchen flinging Smiley-O's and screaming, Dad talking back to NPR and flipping pancakes (today, chocolate chip), and Mom blaring her Zumba DVD in the TV room. So it wasn't exactly like we could have a sane, civilized panel discussion on What to Do If He Calls Back.

Anyway, immediately after breakfast, everyone left. And when Mom finished her shower, she knocked on my door.

"Well?" she said. "So you're probably mad at me for interfering, right? But can I just say something first? I'm not asking for all the gory details, but I knew *something* was going on friendwise. And I'd wanted to have a troop reunion for a long time, regardless. So on Friday, when you came home from school, and I could see you were extremely upset—"

I jumped up from the bed and hugged her. Her body was radiating warmth from the shower, and she smelled like the shampoo version of strawberry. "The troop reunion was great, Mom, really. Don't apologize; I loved it. And thank you."

"Oh," she said, beaming. "Then everything is good with you girls?"

"Everything is great with us girls." I paused. "Not *so* great with the boys."

"Ah, *the boys*," she said. "I don't think s'mores work as well on boys." She laughed. "Although truthfully, I wouldn't know what does. Eighth-grade boys were always a mystery to me."

• • •

Monday morning my stomach felt fluttery, so I just kept reminding myself what Hanna and Olivia had said—that (most of) the girls in the class liked the *Life Cycle*, they thought it was funny and smart, lalala. And even though their approval made me uneasy, at least I could show my face at Fulton Middle School.

And, sure enough, when I walked into homeroom, a bunch of girls led by Dahlia and Sophie immediately swarmed my desk, asking about the science binder.

Where is it now? (Um, home.)

Can we read it? (Um, maybe later.)

Are Dylan and Zachary the only Frogs? (Um, not sure. But it all keeps changing.)

What did you put for Jarret? (Ben, Drew, Kyle, etc.) (Um, don't remember.)

Why did you guys stop writing it? (Um, well. It's kind of a long story. . . .)

The whole time I was answering (or not answering) these questions, Maya sat silently at the desk next to mine, chewing her lower lip. I felt awful that she'd been dragged into this, but I was also wishing she'd chime in with some of the answers.

Meanwhile, from the other side of the room, I could feel Chloe and Sabrina giving me the evil eye.

What were they so mad about? I wondered. Possibly it was Wrath on Behalf of the Boys. Although that would be ironic, considering that (a) they'd always been mean to most of the Croakers and to all of the Tadpoles, and (b) if they truly cared about boy feelings, why did they read my notebook out loud?

As for the boys, they were completely ignoring me. Not looking at me, not talking to me. Literally none of them. Not even Dylan. And not Zachary. But they were huddled together, snickering in a way that creeped me out.

So homeroom that Monday was ubercomplicated. Too much attention, the death stare, the silent treatment—all of it going on at once, from different directions. Kind of the school version of the Davis Chaos, with me as the only Davis.

As soon as the bell rang, I walked straight over to Zachary's desk.

"We need to talk," I announced.

He shrugged. "What about?"

"You called Saturday night? On my cell?"

"I did?" He scratched his nose. "I don't remember. I was kind of busy Saturday night. At a party you invited me to?"

"Yeah, well, sorry about the party, but it turns out I wasn't invited there myself." I was about to explain about Chloe's noninvitation, but Zachary slung his backpack over his shoulder impatiently, like he was in a big hurry to get to science. So I blurted: "And I'm sorry I lied to you about the mnemonics. And I'm *really* sorry if my notebook hurt your feelings. But it was supposed to be private."

"Anything else?"

"What? No. That's a lot to be sorry for."

"Yeah, Finley, it is."

I waited, but he didn't say another word.

"So that's it?" I sputtered. "You're not going to accept my apology? *Any* of them? You're just going to keep making stupid prank calls like a stupid frog?"

"No, I've evolved past phone calls." And he walked off to join Drew Looper and Ben Santino, who slapped his backpack and did the Croaker laugh.

In science that morning we had a test, so at least I didn't need to work on a lab with Zachary. And the next two periods—English and math—also passed without major incidents. By that I mean no interaction with Zachary—which after homeroom was a relief.

But fourth period was art, when we were supposed to turn in our "sunflower-inspired" project. Last night, after sort-of-studying for the eighty millionth quiz on irregular Spanish verbs, I finally took out my sketch pad to draw something unique, something with "character." And I tried to think of an object that was important to me—but the only thing that came to mind was my camera. So I drew my camera in a bunch of different poses—zoom out, zoom in. But every drawing still looked flat, stick-figurey, generic, the opposite of van Gogh's imperfect droopy sunflowers.

And then I thought about my photos, especially the ones I'd taken of Maya, Olivia, and Zachary. They weren't Diane Arbus–good; they weren't anybody-good, not even close. But they weren't cloney or year-booky or fake pretty. And wasn't that the point of the whole assignment? To really see something the way it actually looked?

I answered myself: Why yes, Finley, it was.

Anyhow, for the first time ever in the history of art classes, I actually felt proud of something I'd done. So when Ms. Cronin asked for a volunteer to share their sunflower project, I walked to the front of the studio with my photos of Maya, Olivia, and Zachary.

"I know we were supposed to do a drawing," I said. "But I thought the important thing was to show individual character. So I took these photographs—"

Chloe waved her hand. She didn't wait for Ms. Cronin to call on her. "Finley?" she called out. "You care about *individual character*? I just think that's really so, so fascinating."

Ms. Cronin smiled. "Why, Chloe?"

"Oh, because what Finley is saying—that her photography is like the opposite of stereotyping—is so different from what you'd expect. I mean, based on *other things*."

"I'm not sure I follow," Ms. Cronin said.

Chloe undid her hair clip. "I just meant, you know, the whole idea of treating people *as individuals*—"

"Exactly," Sabrina said. "Human beings."

All of a sudden, I knew exactly where they were going with this—I felt it in my stomach like a cramp. The *Life Cycle* was the opposite of sunflowers. It was all about taking boys and turning them into generic amphibians.

Chloe and Sabrina were right. They were absolutely right, and I had no idea what to answer.

I just stood there, clutching my photos with sweaty

hands, my cheeks burning. And then: "Gggggrrrrkkk."

The sound was faint and muffled, but it was definitely someone croaking into a fist. And it came from the back of the studio. Where Zachary was sitting.

I whipped my head around to stare at him. The corners of his mouth were twitching upward, like he was trying not to smile. And as he stared right back at me, he was barely blinking, just like when he'd lied about the *LUNCH* tattoo.

Thereby proving he was the phantom cell phone croaker.

Not that I'd ever doubted he was, but this non-blinking stare, plus the halfway-hidden smile, definitely proved it.

Well, I refused to let him ruin my art project. I took a breath. "Anyhow," I said loudly. "What I was saying about these photos—"

"Grrrkkk."

Slightly louder now. Was I the only person who could hear this horrible sound? Could I possibly be imagining it? No—because why else would Zachary be not-blinking at me like that?

I locked eyes with Maya, Olivia, Dahlia Ringgold, Ms. Cronin, anyone but Zachary. *Keep talking,* I commanded myself. "I didn't shoot poses, because I think they look too perfect. And I think it's so much more interesting when people don't expect—"

"GRRRRKKKK."

"Ribbit, ribbit."

Now fake-frog noises were popping up from all over the studio. Most of the boys in the class were doing it, and they were grinning, not even trying to hide their mouths behind their fists.

Some girls were starting to giggle.

But not Maya. She jumped out of her seat. "That is just *so rude*," she exclaimed.

Ms. Cronin rapped her desk with some rolled-up sketch paper. "Excuse me, what is going on here, people? In this class, when someone is speaking—"

She went on to patiently explain how the rule was No Ribbiting or Croaking in the Art Studio. When she finally finished, I muttered something about lighting and composition, and dumped the photos on her desk.

"Grrk," someone added.

It could have been Zachary. But I wasn't looking at him then. I was staring at the other boys in the art room.

• • •

After art was lunch. That day Maya and I found a table in the corner, where we were immediately joined by Hanna and Olivia.

Maya was chomping on her veggie taco. She was furious. "I cannot *believe* the boys in this class," she was saying. "Such infants. Such *total moron pea-brained rude jerkwads.*"

"Yeah," I said. "But organized."

"What are you talking about?" Olivia demanded.

I poked the lettuce shreds on my plate. "Have you noticed them today? I mean what they look like."

"Who *cares* what they look like," Maya said. "That's kind of irrelevant, Finley, under the circumstances."

"Not really." I pointed to the table across from ours, where seven boys from our class—including Zachary—were stuffing tacos into their mouths. In art I'd had this feeling about them, but they were scattered all over the studio, so my brain couldn't process all the data. But seeing them together, crammed around the lunch table: That was another thing.

"Look at how they're dressed," I said.

Maya squinted. "What about it?"

"Wait," Hanna said slowly. "They're all wearing

the same colors, aren't they? Greens and browns."

"Yup," I said. "I think they color-coordinated today. To look like frogs."

Olivia burst out laughing. "Okay, Finley, I think you've gone nuts. For starters, boys don't color-coordinate."

"Well, they wear sports uniforms, right?" I argued. "So it's not like they've never heard of colors. And maybe they decided to dress like the Amphibian Team." I waved my arm. "Or something."

"You may be slightly overanalyzing," Hanna said gently. She glanced at the boys' table. "Although I have to admit it *is* a little weird."

"It's more than weird," I insisted. "It's totally on purpose."

Nobody talked. Maya took a big, thoughtful bite of taco, and Olivia sipped her bottled water.

Finally, Hanna said: "Okay, Finley. Even if they all agreed to dress the same—and I think Olivia is right; boys don't *do* stuff like that usually—why would they *want* to dress like the *Life Cycle*? I mean, not to rub it in, but they're obviously mad at you guys."

"Exactly," I agreed. "And it's how they're fighting back. Also why they're croaking."

Maya snapped off teeny bits of taco shell. "Finny, please don't get mad at me for saying this, but that doesn't make any sense, okay? If they were rejecting the *Life Cycle*, they'd be dressed in pink. Or black. Or plaid, or polka dots."

"No," I said. "I think the way they're fighting back is to say, 'Fine, you think we're nothing but amphibians? That's exactly how we're going to act. You talk in class, we'll croak at you. Deal with it. And you can't complain, because this whole frog thing was *your* idea.'"

"That's kind of smart, actually," Hanna said.

"It's warped," Maya corrected her. "And just *rude*. Omigod, Fin. I feel like marching over to that table right now, and—"

"Finley! Move!" Olivia squealed.

Too late. A jabbing poke to my shoulder, then suddenly a wave of coldness and wetness splashing across my neck, the collar of my shirt, my back.

I gasped and spun around.

Zachary, Drew, and Ben were standing behind me, laughing. And Zachary was waving a two-thirds-full bottle of water.

"Are you insane?" I screeched. "You just poured *water* on me?"

"Water is our natural habitat," Zachary explained in a Dr. Science voice, grinning in a way that was uber-Tadpole. "We're still developing. Sorry if we're a little clumsy."

Across the cafeteria Mr. Coffee was texting. Instead of noticing.

Maya jumped up and snatched the bottle. "You know what?" she hissed at Zachary. "You're just as obnoxious as you were last year, and the year before that, and the year before that. You haven't changed *one single iota*. I'm sorry we were ever nice to you. And you never deserved Finley's crush!"

"What?" he said, as his goofy smile faded. "What are you—"

"Nothing," I growled. "Delete that last comment, all right?"

Meanwhile, Hanna and Olivia had grabbed some greasy napkins from the table and were blotting my back. But it was all unbearable—not just the wetness and the taco grease on my neck, I mean the whole scene: the lunchroom buzzing, everyone staring, the three boys standing there stupidly. And especially Maya's public-service announcement about my crush.

So I got up from the table and ran. Just ran.

CHAPTER 19

I ended up in the second floor girls' room, which was empty, luckily. So I banged on the automatic hand dryer and crouched below it, the hot air whooshing down my spine.

A gazillion emotions pinballed in my brain:

Fury at Maya for blurting about my (former) crush. To my (former) crush.

Gratitude that she had my back—literally and figuratively.

Shock at Zachary's moronic, immature prank.

Humiliation, because the whole grade was watching.

Frustration, because I needed to respond now, obviously. And I had no idea how.

But while the noisy heat attacked my cotton T-shirt, I decided three things:

1) Whatever-I-did had to be right away. In the last two days, Zachary had croak-called me, organized a frog color day at school, ribbited at me in class, and splashed water down my back. I needed to come up with something fast, before he thought of a prank even more obnoxious.

2) Whatever-I-did had to be public. I'd tried talking to Zachary in private twice, to explain and apologize, and he would barely make eye contact. Clearly he wanted to play Croaker hero, and if he was conducting his war in public, I needed to respond in front of the entire class.

3) Whatever-I-did couldn't just be words. Zachary was doing Stuff—so I had to do Stuff right back. Besides, the *Life Cycle* was nothing but words, and look where words had gotten me.

Irk, I thought. The *Life Cycle.* The cause of all of this disaster.

The hand dryer turned off. I stared at myself in the mirror.

Why had we compared boys to amphibians in the first place? If only we'd picked adorable little kittens, say, I wouldn't be in this mess. The truth was, I didn't remember a whole lot about frog development. So how could I come up with some sort of frog-themed payback that was better than *Grrkk, ribbit, oops, I'm so clumsy with bottled water*?

I squirted soap foam on my hands, turned on the faucet, and slowly rubbed my palms together.

And a funny thing happened then. You know how you get a song stuck in your head sometimes, and you don't know where it comes from? As I stood in front of the mirror washing my hands, I suddenly had a flashback to the word "kerfuffle" and what Ms. Krieger had said to me that day in the library: *What do we do, Finley, when we don't know something?*

Look it up.

A minute later I burst through the library doors, and was immediately pounced on by Maya, Hanna, and Olivia.

"Where were you?" Maya shouted. "I was sure you'd come here straight from the lunchroom. Are you okay?"

"I needed to dry off first," I said. "But I'm fine. Listen."

I told them what I'd decided: We needed froggy-themed retaliation, but it couldn't be as lame as what the boys were doing. It had to prove we knew something about amphibians. It couldn't be generic or obvious. And it had to be quick.

"But if we do something," Hanna said (and I smiled a little when she said "we"), "won't that just encourage them to do more stuff back? Maybe if we just ignored them—"

"Not possible," I insisted.

"Or if you explained about the *Life Cycle*—"

"Also not possible. Believe me, Hanna, I tried. I also apologized, but Zachary won't listen. He just wants to make this a stupid game."

Maya's eyes glowed. She loved games. And she was the most competitive person I knew. "All right, so what should we do?"

"I think we should brainstorm," I said. "After we've done a little research."

Ms. Krieger's ears must have perked up at the word "research." From her computer by the circulation desk she said, "Girls? You'll let me know if you need any help?"

"Actually . . . ," I said, grinning.

• • •

We spent the rest of lunch in the library, Olivia and Hanna flipping through nature books, Maya and me reading stuff online. The funny thing was how Ms. Krieger was all, *Oh yes indeedy, it's no big deal for eighth-grade girls to come bursting into my inner sanctum demanding information about amphibian eating habits.* She didn't ask any of the typical questions you'd expect from grown-ups—*Oh, did one of you get a pet tadpole? Oh, are you studying frogs in science? Oh, is this some sort of wacky, madcap scavenger hunt?* She just pointed out the shelf for amphibians and reptiles, asked if any of us wanted tea (which that day she pronounced "tay"), and then disappeared inside her office to play Guatemalan flute music.

So we researched amphibians without needing to invent some cheesy grown-up-friendly explanation. And in the ten minutes or so until it was time for Spanish, I scribbled these notes—this time in my social studies binder:

Frogs eat bugs, snails, spiders, worms, and small fish. Some just eat bugs.
Snakes, foxes, dogs, bass, pike, hawks & seagulls eat frogs.

Frogs: no teeth.

Tongues = sticky.

Bulging eyes on top of head see in different directions. Eyes sink thru openings in their skulls, forcing food down throats. "Blink" while eating.

"Brilliant," Maya commented, reading over my shoulder. "Gorgeous, disgusting, mesmerizing. Wanna hear what I got?"

"Sure."

She read aloud from her monitor: "*Frogs drink water with their skin, not their mouths. A group of frogs is called an army.*"

"Seriously?" Olivia said, walking over to the computer desks. "I thought a group of frogs was a school."

"A group of *fish* is a school," Maya corrected her. "And that includes tadpoles. Whereas frogs form *armies*."

"Well, silly me," Olivia said. She tapped on her book. "Okay, so listen to this: *You can distinguish frog genders by noting the relative size of their ears. Frogs' ears are located right behind their eyes. If its ears are as big as its eyes, it's a male. If its ears are smaller than its eyes, it's a female.*"

"Whoa, fascinating," Maya said, laughing. "And it totally explains Zachary's huge sticking-out ears."

"Which he doesn't have anymore," Hanna said quickly.

"Oh yes, he does," I said. "He just grew his hair longer, to cover them."

"Right," Maya agreed. "He hasn't changed, Hanna; he's just hiding things better. What did you get?"

"Not much," Hanna said, flipping through her book. "It's a myth that frogs give you warts. Frogs are cold-blooded, they hibernate in winter, blah blah. Oh, but *this* is interesting. Did you know that only the male frog croaks?"

"Seriously?" Maya said. She seemed offended. "You're saying female frogs don't even communicate? They just sit there boringly on their lily pads and—"

"No, Maya, will you please shut up? Females communicate when they have something to say—they make distress calls. But male frogs croak just for the sake of croaking."

"Because males like sound effects," I said, then immediately realized I was talking exactly like Mom.

• • •

In Spanish Señor Hansen gave us another test, only this one was an essay on "My First Day of School." To write it you had to use the preterit, switching sometimes to the imperfect, so I didn't have tons to say on this subject. In fact, after about three minutes I ran out of verbs I was semisure how to conjugate, so I started doodling frog eyes.

And thinking: *Frog eyes are weird. Maybe the weirdest thing about frogs, really. Especially that eating thing: the way they force food down by blinking. Sort of a cross between cool and disgusting. Also the way they catch bugs on their tongues—that's cool and disgusting, too.*

On the back of the exam I wrote this list:

Possible Payback Themes
1—Something with frog eyes?
2—Something with eating?
3—Something with bugs?

Unfortunately, Señor Hansen snatched my exam before I could erase these questions.

"Once again, I see we're focusing on Spanish," he sneered.

CHAPTER 20

The next morning Maya, Olivia, and Hanna were waiting at my locker.

"So?" Olivia said eagerly. "Is there a plan yet?"

Maya grinned. "Hey, I've got one. What about hopping?"

"Hopping?" I repeated, as I unbuttoned my jacket. "How is that a plan?"

"We could randomly hop, just spontaneously leap out of our chairs whenever we felt like it. You know, like frogs."

Hanna patted Maya's shoulder. "You *would* think of something like that, Maya."

"Right, I would. Because it's brilliant."

"Okay, but how is it payback?" I said. "I mean, I get that hopping is froglike, but—"

"Or we could hop on cue," Maya offered. "Like every time a boy went 'ribbit.' Or every time a boy acted like an immature jerk."

Olivia laughed. "Then we'd be hopping nonstop, Maya. And I'm not sure teachers like Hansen would be too thrilled."

"Oh. Well, if we're caring about *Señor Hansen* . . ." Maya rolled her eyes.

"What about dying our hair green," Olivia suggested. "Not with permanent dye or anything. Just to outdo the boys on the color-coordination thing."

"Ooh, I love that, actually," Maya said. "Green hair is awesome."

"But it's not revenge," I protested. "It doesn't *say* anything. It doesn't show we *know* anything. Also, frankly it's a bit St. Patrick's Day."

"You have a better idea?" Maya challenged me. She crossed her arms.

"No," I admitted. "I've been thinking about frog food, but I'm not there yet. What about you, Hanna?"

She nodded. "Warts," she said, beaming.

• • •

Warts. That was it. Everyone fell passionately in love with warts.

And even though warts-from-frogs were only a myth, and not scientific fact, which had been the whole point of going to the library, I had to agree that warts were better than green hair and hopping. Hanna's idea was: Since we'd come in contact with amphibian boys over the years, sitting next to them in classes, banging into them at the lockers, and occasionally even holding their hands, we now had these (awful but fake) warts on our faces and fingers. Ha ha.

Not exactly payback for the croaking and the water down my back. But whatever. Warts told the boys: *You are all froglike specimens, stuck somewhere in the tadpole–frog life cycle. And see the effect you've had on us girls? Eww.*

And anyhow, it was now obvious that we needed to do something—anything—immediately. That morning, the boys had shown up wearing swim goggles over their eyes. A few of the boys (Jonathan, Cody, even Wyeth) wore the goggles on top of their heads, which I had to admit looked vaguely amphibian.

But it was Ben Santino who grabbed everyone's

attention, because he showed up to school in a black wet suit, a snorkel and mask, and orange flippers. He made this sort of Darth Vader noise as he breathed through his snorkel, and as he walked up and down the hall, his feet smacked the floor in an irrelevant walrus-type way. But even so, the whole costume still said *water-inhabiting creature*, and by second period the entire school was giggling hysterically.

In art Chloe announced, "Don't you love it? Isn't Ben hilarious? I guess *certain people* are wishing they could take back what they wrote."

"Well, too late," Sabrina said, smirking. "Because they can't."

All day long, no one could stop pointing at the boys, talking about how cute they looked in goggles, how funny Ben was in his costume. Only Señor Hansen was unimpressed.

"No swim gear in Spanish class," he declared, as if he were reciting a passage from the Fulton Middle School Code of Behavior.

I went straight home after basketball practice, determined to come up with warts—gross, misshapen, deformed-looking warts that no one could ignore, especially the boys. Luckily, our house was full of art supplies, so the first thing I did was open the kitchen pantry, which was where Mom stashed the Terribles' No Worries Organic Play-Clay.

The big trick was getting the warts to look like warts and not zits. Which meant they needed to be round but not smooth, and any color other than pink or red. I also needed to find a way to make the warts stick to our faces and hands. But I was sure I could come up with something—Mom wasn't just obsessed with Play-Doh alternatives; she was also a big believer in all-natural adhesive alternatives, so the Terribles had a huge supply of pastes, glues, tape, and other sticky substances sent in sample sizes by companies hoping to earn Mom's Chemical-Free Mommy Seal of Approval.

That afternoon at least I had the house to myself, because Mom had taken the Terribles to Gymboree. So I was able to focus on the Play-Clay, which was a faded yellowy-brownish color, sort of a compromise between my own paleness, Maya's olive skin, Hanna's pinkness, and Olivia's cocoa brown, but decent enough for all-purpose warts, I guessed. I rolled some clay between my fingers, made about fifteen warts of various shapes and sizes, turned on the oven to 275 degrees, then placed the warts on an ungreased cookie sheet, just like the Play-Clay canister instructed.

At five-fifteen Mom, Max, and Addie burst through the door.

"BOOMZOOM," Max shouted, as he came crashing into the kitchen, followed by Addie, who immediately spotted the open canister of No Worries on the counter.

"Finnee, play dat?" she asked, pointing excitedly.

"Sorry, Addie, I wish I could, but tons of homework," I answered. "Where's Mom?"

"Schlepping groceries from the car," Mom announced, panting a little as she walked into the kitchen and dumped a cloth tote bag on the counter. "I could really use some help, Fin, honey."

"Oh, sure." I went out to the driveway to get two more overflowing bags from the Toddler Mobile. And on the way back inside I spotted a small pizza box on our front step.

That was funny. We almost never ordered pizza; whenever we had pizza at our house, it was usually because Dad made an entire pie from scratch. Besides, this box was big enough for a single slice, maybe two— and we were the kind of family who always ordered family-size. I mean, the rare times when we ordered pizza.

I rested the bags on the step. Then I reached down to pick up the pizza box, which had obviously been littered there sometime since I'd gotten home from school. Who would do such a thing? How disgusting: Litter anywhere was bad enough, but litter dumped in front of your house was truly repulsive, I thought.

All of a sudden, the pizza box twitched.

I shrieked and dropped it on the step.

Out raced a tiny frog. AN ACTUAL FROG.

"Finny, you all right?" Mom was at the door holding a cucumber, which presumably she intended to use to fight off marauding attackers.

"Absolutely fine," I sputtered. "Someone delivered a frog."

"Delivered?"

"As a joke. An idiot boy in my class. Probably a bunch of idiot boys." *An army,* I told myself.

"Well, that's not funny," Mom said indignantly. "It's way too cold out here for frogs."

She handed me the cucumber. Then she squatted behind the step and started groping around in the frozen soil behind the pachysandra bushes.

"Want some help?" I asked doubtfully.

"No, Finny, I've got this," she said, frowning.

A second later she was beaming, showing me the tiny creature clasped in her hands.

Right away Mom went into troop-leader mode.

"Finley, there are some ancient mason jars on the top shelf in the left cabinet," she announced. "Get one down, wash it in that new veggie-based soap I'm reviewing, and then poke some holes in the lid with fork prongs."

"Prong!" Max shouted. He was spinning like a top.

"Yes, prong," Mom repeated distractedly. "And we'll need some food for the little guy. Remember that Green Girls badge we did, Finley, on animal habitats? I'm trying to remember what frogs eat."

"Bugs, snails, spiders, worms, and small fish," I blurted. Mom raised her eyebrows. "But mostly bugs," I added casually, poking the lid with a fork.

"Impressive you remember that," Mom said.

"Yeah," I said. "Even without a mnemonic."

She smiled. "Well, I'm sure we can get some bugs at Pet World tomorrow morning. But I wish we could feed him something right now. He's probably traumatized, poor little thing. All shut up in that dark cold pizza box—"

"Frogs hibernate during the winter, so he should be fine," I said. "And why are we assuming it's a he? Did you compare the relative eye and ear size? Or hear croaking? Because it could be a female."

"Yes, of course," Mom said. She gently dropped the tiny frog into the jar and screwed on the lid. "You sure do know a lot about frogs," she commented, scooping up Addie to give her a peek.

"Not really," I said.

"I WANNA HOLD," Addie shouted, squirming.

"No, sweetie, we're going to let the little froggy rest quietly in her jar," Mom said.

"Or his," I said.

"Or his." Mom's face brightened. "I know. Why don't we all think of a good name."

"Little Teeny," Addie said. "Barbie."

"Prong," Max said.

Mom's eyes met mine, and we burst out laughing.

She kissed Max's curly head. "Prong," she agreed. "Although, really, it's Finley's frog, so she should decide."

"Who says it's mine?" I argued.

"It was a gift," Mom said. "Delivered to your doorstep by a bunch of silly boys. Or *one* boy in particular. Right?"

"Yeah, right," I muttered. "But Prong is fine with me." My cheeks were heating up. Although the kitchen was warm, so that was probably the reason.

And just at that moment Mom's face puckered. "Hey, is that the oven I'm smelling? Are you baking something, Finley?"

"Oh, right. Warts," I said.

"*Warts?* I'm sorry, did you just say—"

"Science project." And then I jumped up to rescue the cookie tray.

CHAPTER 21

When Dad got home that evening, Mom was putting the twins to bed. So I showed him Prong, and the first thing Dad said was, "But what do we feed him?"

I'm not joking. Seriously, it was like both my parents were obsessed with frog nutrition. Or maybe they didn't want to face the Amphibian Police: *So. You're claiming that after some Stupid Unnamed Boys in Finley's class dumped this innocent little frog on your doorstep (in a pizza box, no less) you let him/her go an* entire night *without a properly balanced frog meal? And you call yourselves* responsible parents?

"I really think this guy could use some bugs," Dad remarked.

"It's possibly a she," I said. "And Mom says she'll get some in the morning. At the pet store."

"I'm not sure we should wait until the morning," Dad said. "He's not acting very energetic."

"Because he or she is *in a jar*," I said. "And hibernating, right? Dad, you think it should be practicing hook shots in there?"

"Don't be so hilarious, Finster," he said, messing my hair. "I'm just saying that in my learned opinion, the little fella is hungry."

He left the kitchen. A few minutes later he came back with a strip of orange-brown sticky-looking paper that smelled like rotting apples. If you looked closely at the strip, you could see flies. Whole flies and fly parts, mostly wing fragments, dried up like ashes.

"Eww," I said. "What *is* that thing?"

"Flypaper," Dad replied. "Some nice green company sent Mom like a dozen boxes of the stuff to review on her blog last summer. It's a bit old-school, but a totally safe, nontoxic alternative to pesticides and bug sprays." He sniffed it and made a face. "A few months ago I hung a strip next to the furnace, and now we have a home-cooked meal for Froggy."

"Prong," I corrected Dad, as he pried the fly bits off the sticky paper with the same fork I'd used to poke holes. I watched while he lowered the fly food into the jar. No way was Prong going to eat that junk, I decided. Not when it was so sticky and gross-smelling.

On the other hand, I thought, *huh.* This flypaper stuff worked. It did catch bugs.

Just the way frogs caught bugs with their sticky tongues. A scientific fact you could look up online, or in the Fulton Middle School library.

And yes, the flypaper was sticky and gross-smelling. But also the right combination of harmless and disgusting. Organic, too.

Soooo . . . in other words, perfect.

The totally perfect froggy-themed payback!

Woo-hoo!

I twirled around the kitchen while Dad looked at me with an expression like, *Middle school girls. Sheesh.*

That night Mom wrote a blog post about how boys thought in straight lines (you use a fork to poke holes in a jar lid, so your son names the new pet frog Prong). Whereas girls, according to her, thought in squiggles—

you were pretty sure you could follow the direction of their thought process, when suddenly, oops, the next thing you know, boys are leaving them frogs in pizza boxes and they're baking warts on cookie sheets.

I mean, that was the gist. Mom titled the post "Lines and Squiggles." She asked for comments, but I forced myself not to write anything *(Excuse me? Squiggles? What? Love, Awesome Daughter)*.

Instead what I did was text Maya, Hanna, and Olivia: *Meet at lockers @ 7am tmrw.* I knew they'd assume we needed time to glue on the warts, so they wouldn't question the early arrival.

On Wednesday morning, I scribbled Mom and Dad a note to say I needed to get to school early "for my science project." Then I peeled a banana for breakfast and checked on Prong. Somehow he/she had made it through the night, even without sampling any fly cuisine.

Well, I told Prong as I put the jar back on the kitchen counter, *I hope you like pet-store bugs better. And spring is just a few weeks away, so hang in there, okay?*

On the way out, I grabbed all dozen boxes of fly-paper and crammed them into one of Mom's cotton tote bags.

By the time I got to school, Maya, Olivia and Hanna were waiting at my locker. Surprisingly, Dahlia Ringgold and Sophie Yang were there too.

"They want to join the festivities," Maya explained, grinning. "I told them there were warts involved, and they just said, 'Yay, we love warts.'"

"We did," Sophie insisted. "We do."

"And the boys, it's really *so obnoxious*," Dahlia added. "It's just like, I don't know. The way they're acting." She shook her head.

"Great," I said. "The more the merrier. Except we're not doing the warts."

Maya's face fell. "Oh no. You couldn't make them?"

"No, I could. I even baked a whole batch. But I thought of something even better. Voilà."

I dumped the boxes of flypaper on the floor.

"We'll decorate lockers," I said. "With sticky, gross-smelling flypaper. *Which catches bugs exactly like a frog tongue*," I added, in case anyone wasn't following.

"Whoa," Olivia said. "That's definitely payback."

And Dahlia said, "I mean it's just so incredibly . . ." Her eyes popped.

"Um, Finley?" Hanna said slowly. "Not to wimp

out on you or anything, but don't you think this may be a little . . . extreme?" She exchanged glances with Olivia. "I mean, except for the water bottle, which I agree was totally over the line, all the boys did was croak and ribbit. And wear green clothes and goggles. But seriously, *flypaper* . . . ?"

"They dumped a frog on my front step," I announced. "A cute little helpless *frog*, Hanna. In a dirty old pizza box."

"*What?*" Maya said.

"Yesterday afternoon. We put it in a jar."

Maya was literally jumping. "That's APPALLING."

"I know, right?" I said. "My baby brother named it Prong. It's extremely adorable, by the way."

"Okay," Hanna said. "Dumping a frog was wrong, I'm not arguing. But the thing is, you guys, I agreed to warts. I *thought* of warts. And putting that flypaper stuff on people's lockers is sort of vandalism."

"Oh, but it's not," I protested. "It's actually the *opposite* of vandalism; if it attracts bugs, it's helping the janitors *clean the school*, if you think about it. Plus this flypaper is one hundred percent safe, organic, and nontoxic," I added, pointing to the box.

"Except to the bugs," Olivia said.

"Well, yes. Except to the bugs."

"I don't know," Hanna said, sighing.

"Well, you don't have to decide anything right now, anyway," I said. Before anyone else, specifically Olivia, could agree with Hanna, I explained that it didn't make sense to attach the flypaper before the end of the school day; if we wanted maximum bug attraction, it needed to work overnight.

I unzipped my backpack and revealed a box of graham crackers, some marshmallows, and some Hershey bars, all the leftovers from the s'mores. After we'd decorated certain lockers with flypaper, I said, we'd sprinkle a few crumbs on the sticky surfaces for good measure. Because one thing I'd remembered from Green Girls campouts—bugs appreciated sugar as much as we did.

"Hee hee, fabutastic," Maya said. "This is so sick, Finley. I love it!" And then she did a perfect cartwheel.

The real challenge was getting through the school day without letting the boys know anything was up. So when they croaked at us—which they did constantly, sometimes softly, sometimes loudly, especially in the hallways—we had to act like we couldn't hear, didn't notice, didn't care. And I know people say, *Oh, just ignore it,* when someone teases or bullies, but that's pretty worthless advice, if you ask me. When almost the entire grade of boys is ribbiting whenever you walk past, ignoring is not an option. But you can *pretend* to ignore it—at least, you can fake-ignore it for a few hours.

Plus I could tell Zachary was waiting for me to say something about yesterday's frog delivery—confront him, maybe yell at him, try again to "talk." But I resisted all of the above. I had to sit next to Zachary in science and Spanish, but I didn't have to look at him, I told myself. Or smell his laundry detergent. Or peek at his drawings. Or even listen to his foot going *tap-tap-tap* and wonder if he was nervous about something, and what that something could be. Considering he was the Croaker hero, general of the Croaker army, it was pretty hard to imagine what he could be nervous about. Not that I cared, anyway.

At basketball practice, Sabrina Leftwich said it was her duty as captain to give the team a pep talk. Except it wasn't a pep talk at all. It was more like a rant: *It's really upsetting to me, you guys, when I feel like I'm the only one who's giving my all at practice, while some of you*—here she made eye contact with me—*are not totally committed to the team, lalala.* Sophie Yang (who up until this morning I'd assumed was a generic Chloe-team follower) made a noise like barfing. And it was really impressive, because she did it without moving her mouth or even changing her expression.

When Sabrina finally finished ranting, Sophie, Dahlia, and I raced to the lockers. Hanna had decided not to do the flypaper; she'd be the lookout, she said, which I realized was a good idea. The school was surprisingly busy at that hour, and we needed to be sure no one would walk by while we decorated.

Meanwhile, Maya was wrestling with the flypaper boxes. "Finally!" she shouted at us. "What took you guys so long? I've been trying to open these without getting stuck."

"Slow down," I told her. "First we should probably decide which lockers we're decorating."

"Zachary's," Maya said right away.

Everyone nodded. *Ooh, yeah. Definitely Zachary's!*

"Drew and Ben," Olivia said. "Jarret and Kyle."

"Jonathan Pressman," Dahlia said. Then she laughed. "Wyeth Brockman."

"What? No," I blurted.

"No?" Maya squinted at me. "You're vetoing Wyeth? Seriously?"

"Yeah," I said. "I'll explain later, okay?"

She shrugged one shoulder. "Fine. Then I'm vetoing Dylan."

I would have said, *Oh, but Dylan is different from Wyeth. Wyeth is not a* crush; *he's just a nice kid who was nice to me when I needed niceness.* But we didn't have time for one of our big Finley-Maya arguments. I carefully ripped open a box.

"Gug," Olivia said, her face pinching. "That stuff smells like nail-polish remover."

"To me it smells like rotting apples," I said cheerfully. "Let's start with Zachary."

The hard part was figuring how to attach it. Flypaper, it turned out, was supposed to be suspended from the ceiling, just sort of fluttering in the breeze as bugs drunkenly crashed into it. And we definitely wanted that bug-catching effect, but we also wanted to wrap the door of Zachary's locker, the way I'd wrapped Maya's for her birthday. So in the end what we did was coil five flypapers into a big messy blob and make a sort of abstract art-sculpture thingy, a tangle of rotting-apple stickiness that would need to be pried off with an ice pick. Really, it looked so impressive that I was sorry I hadn't brought my camera.

The other boys' lockers we did much faster—just one flypaper roll per locker door, twisted in a sort of free-form squashed pretzel. And we had just finished Jarret's door when I realized that Maya wasn't standing with us there to admire it.

"Where's Maya?" I said.

"She said she needed to step out for a minute," Hanna answered. Her eyes darted down the hallway. "Please hurry up, you guys, okay? My mom just texted. She said the roads are getting slippery and she's coming to get me."

I thought it was odd that Maya had taken off without explaining, but it wasn't the most unpredictable thing she'd done lately. We waited another five minutes for her to return, but when we heard teacher voices in the hallway—and one of the voices belonged to Señor Hansen—we decided we couldn't hang around any longer. It was too dangerous. Our lookout was leaving. The roads were getting bad. And truthfully, by then the smell of rotting apples was pretty nauseating.

CHAPTER 22

In Fulton it snows a lot. It doesn't bother us, usually—we plow the roads, shovel our driveways, dress in plenty of layers. And because we're all so expert at dealing with snow, we never get snow days. Except that Thursday they declared an *ice* day, on account of slippery roads that the school-bus company called a hazard.

To me this was torture. For the first time ever in the history of school attendance I was desperate to go—but I consoled myself with the thought that the extra day meant extra bugs on the boys' lockers.

That morning my cell rang four times. First Olivia

called to repeat everything that had happened yesterday ("And wasn't it smart for Hanna to stand guard at the lockers? And wasn't it weird how Maya just disappeared?"). Then Drew Looper called to croak, followed by Zachary and someone who snickered like Jarret, so that meant it was either Jarret or Kyle. Possibly both. *How weird the world has gotten,* I thought. *Ice day in Fulton. Zachary croaking with his former nemesis. Nemeses,* if that was the plural.

"Aren't you guys sick of croaking?" I said to them. "Can't you come up with *anything* more creative? I mean, seriously, it's like you're not even trying."

No answer.

So I hung up.

Then Maya called.

"Ice day," she said happily. "Can you believe it, Finley?"

"I'm capable of believing anything at this point," I told her. "Zachary and Jarret just called me together, which I'm pretty sure means it's the Apocalypse."

"They *called* you?"

"Just to ribbit. So where did you go yesterday?"

"It's a surprise," Maya answered.

"It is? You mean for me?"

"Not for *you*, but I'm sure you'll like it. Can I say something?"

"No one could stop you, Maya."

"True." She breathed into the phone. "Okay. So when we were decorating the lockers yesterday? It made me think how I trashed your birthday collage. But I only did that because you hurt my feelings."

"I know," I said. "I wasn't even mad about it. Besides, it was time. The paper was getting all scraggly."

"Yeah, a little. But I'm still sorry I threw it in the trash. It was beautiful." She sighed. "Anyhow, I'm just so glad we finally stopped fighting. And that you stopped being such a boy wimp."

Here we go again, I thought. *A hug and a pinch. Maya acting superior.*

On the other hand, I realized she was right—I'd been a sort of boy wimp, boringly sitting on my lily pad. And now here I was devising payback. So what she said was actually a compliment.

"Um, thank you," I said.

"Um, you're welcome," she replied.

Then my text-message sound went off. It was from Zachary and it said: *ribbitribbit.*

• • •

On Friday morning, Mrs. Lopez drove Maya and me to school. We wanted to be sure to get there early, so we wouldn't miss anyone's reaction. I even brought my camera, because something told me the boys wouldn't be doing generic yearbook-type expressions when they witnessed their sticky lockers.

And I can't say that I expected Zachary to greet us with a white flag, surrounded by his Croaker army, all of them declaring in unison: *Okay, you won, we acknowledge your superior prank-itude, we hereby end this stupid competition, we even forgive you for your stupid notebook.* Followed by all of us—not just me, but Maya, Hanna, Olivia, Sophie, and Dahlia—helping the boys pry off the flypaper. Maybe even followed by a yummy snack of s'mores.

Instead we were greeted with this: Mr. Lundquist, the school janitor, scraping Zachary's locker and muttering under his breath. Señor Hansen standing to the janitor's right, making a unibrow. Ms. Fisher-Greenglass to the janitor's left, typing into her phone.

As soon as we walked in, she looked up and smiled tightly. "Good morning, girls. Welcome back. Did you have a nice day off?"

Maya and I nodded.

"Good," she said. "So. Do either or both of you girls know anything about these locker doors?"

"Miss Lopez does," Señor Hansen sneered. "She sneaked into my classroom with the same vile material."

"What?" I said.

Maya glanced at me. Her face had splotched pink.

"I believe the intent was to vandalize my desk," Señor Hansen declared in a weirdly formal voice, as if he'd morphed into Sherlock Holmes. "As it happened, I was working late that afternoon, grading quizzes. But I stepped outside my classroom for a moment, and when I returned, Miss Lopez was standing at my desk. She made an excuse about needing a Spanish-English dictionary, which I found difficult to believe. Then she ran out, as if she was trying to flee, so I took the opportunity to inspect my classroom." He waved one scary-hairy hand at Zachary's locker. "And discovered this same *extremely* unpleasant material on the seats of two classmates."

"You said Chloe and Sabrina," Ms. Fisher-Greenglass said, typing.

"Miss DeGenidis and Miss Leftwich," he repeated. "Exactly. Miss Lopez has had some friction with these girls in the past. As you are well aware she has had with me."

"Yes, I'm aware." Ms. Fisher-Greenglass looked up; her eyes were serious, almost sad. "Maya, let's take a walk to my office, shall we?"

"You mean right now?" Maya asked faintly.

"Don't worry, I'll inform your homeroom teacher." The principal clamped her hand on Maya's shoulder, and the two of them left the lockers.

All I could do was stand there hopelessly, listening to the *scrape-scrape-scrape* of Mr. Lundquist's knife. And maybe because I was in shock, I peeked at the flypaper on Zachary's locker—which seemed housefly-free. It hadn't even worked, apparently. But it still smelled horrible.

"*Tu amiga tiene una problema grande,*" Senor Hansen said. He smiled fiendishly, flashing his teeth.

It was the first Spanish sentence I ever understood perfectly.

Maya didn't show up for homeroom, or for first-period science, or for any other class that morning. She was clearly in trouble—*grande* trouble, because this was her second offense against Señor Hansen, and it involved not only lockers and chairs, but also Señor Hansen's desk. (That is, according to Señor Hansen.)

Of course I realized I was in trouble too. So were Olivia, Hanna, Sophie, and Dahlia, but maybe not as much trouble as me.

Although me not as much as Maya.

Who beat me in everything, it seemed. Even trouble.

I admit I was mad at her for not sticking to the plan. The flypaper was supposed to be for frog payback, not Señor Hansen payback, or Chloe-and-Sabrina payback. And running off by herself to Señor Hansen's classroom was incredibly risky. It almost seemed as if she was asking to be caught. Asking us all to be caught.

And taking on Señor Hansen, of all people? Again?

Was she insane?

All signs pointed to yes, absolutely. And incredibly dumb, too—because as soon as Maya's parents found out about the Señor Hansen business, they'd yank her out of gymnastics, which she cared about more than anything.

But.

I still felt responsible. The flypaper had been

my idea. The *Life Cycle* had mostly been mine. And if it hadn't been for my stupid carelessness, Chloe wouldn't have stolen my notebook, and nobody would have heard about what I'd written, and then Zachary wouldn't have started his war against us, and I wouldn't have had to come up with froggy-themed payback.

Plus Maya was anti–*Life Cycle*—but even so, she'd told the class she'd cowritten all the entries; she'd rescued the notebook from Chloe and Sabrina; she'd joined my side the second the boys started their croak-calling. She never hesitated; she always had my back.

And there was this, which I hadn't let myself think about before, but which I needed to now: Way before everything got messy and complicated, Maya liked Zachary. I mean, we never discussed it, but it was obvious. And when she thought that I possibly liked him too, she stepped aside. She even did what she could to help me—she set me up to take his photo, to go with him to Chloe's party. Of course, I didn't appreciate her interference, but that wasn't the point—what I needed to remember was that she'd been looking after me.

The thing was, Maya and I had been through a

lot these past two weeks—one kerfuffle after another. But we were best friends. That would never change— not in middle school, not in high school. So I couldn't abandon her now, with her *problema grande*.

The only question was: How could I help her?

I could think of just one way. It wasn't brilliant, and it probably wouldn't work, but it was the single idea my brain could come up with at that moment.

So at lunch I escaped from the building.

Mom was in the kitchen reading *The Sneetches* to the Terribles when I burst into the house.

"Finley? Is that you?" she called.

"Just forgot something," I panted, clutching my science notebook. "Mom."

"Yes."

"Could you possibly—would it be possible?" Oh great, now I was sounding like Dahlia Ringgold.

"Yes?" Mom looked alarmed. "Could I what?"

"Drive me back to school? Now?"

I must have had a demented expression on my face, because she didn't even ask what was going on. She just plopped the Terribles into their car seats and pulled the Toddler Mobile out of the driveway.

"Finnee, where are you here?" Addie asked incomprehensibly.

But Mom just said, "Not now, Addie," in a voice that meant *not now*. Then she stuck on a Wiggles tape to occupy the twins' brainlets.

"Mom," I said. "Has the principal called you?"

"No. Should I be expecting a call?"

"Yeah, I'm pretty sure you should."

"About?"

I took a quick breath. "Okay. You remember the frog delivery? And the warts?"

"Ah yes. The warts." She checked her rearview mirror. "Your science project, right?"

"It wasn't exactly a science project. Well, it was *sort* of one."

"Keep talking."

"Okay. There's been all this boy-versus-girl stuff at school. Really immature, I mean from the boys. And I did a prank. The whole ex-troop did, but it was my idea. As a way of retaliating for Prong." I told her about the flypaper, but not about Maya's independent project. Because that was Mrs. Lopez's business, I decided. "Anyhow, Ms. Fisher-Greenglass saw the lockers this morning, and she wasn't happy. So."

"So," Mom said.

"I wanted to tell you. First. Before she called you."

Mom drove without saying a word. Then she pulled up to the school.

"You know, you can tell me anything," she said quietly.

"I can?" I stared at her. "Then you're not mad at me?"

"Well, sure, I'm *mad*. Vandalizing school property? Finley honey, that's rotten judgment. And you deserve whatever punishment Ms. Fisher-Greenglass gives you."

"Okay. I mean, I know that."

"And of course there'll also be a punishment for you at home."

"I figured. You can take my Christmas camera. I probably failed that Spanish test anyway."

"You did?" Mom gave the steering wheel a light slap. "Okay, that's it, we're getting you a tutor!"

I looked up hopefully. "My punishment is a Spanish tutor?"

"No, Finley, the tutor is a *gift*. Taking away your camera is the *punishment*."

"Oh. No, sure, of course."

"But I'm glad you told me," Mom added, sighing. "I'm glad you knew you could." She leaned over and kissed my cheek. "You'd better get to class now, Awesome Daughter."

I got out of the car. "Thanks, Mom," I said.

"Anytime." Then she winked at me. "Boys are *w-e-i-r-d*," she spelled, and drove off.

CHAPTER 23

I grabbed Zachary's arm just as he was leaving the lunchroom. "Come with me," I commanded. "Now."

And I guess he was too shocked to refuse or to make a joke. But when he saw where we were headed, he asked, "What about Spanish?"

"I've got that covered," I told him. "This is more important."

I pushed open the door of the school library.

"Ms. Krieger," I said. "Could I please talk to Zachary here for a second? In private?"

She perched her lime-green glasses on top of her head. "Five minutes, Finley," she murmured. "Tops.

I'll write you guys a note, but that's my limit."

"Thank you."

"De rien."

I led Zachary to the red sofa.

"Can I ask you something?" he said. "What was that stuff you put on my locker?"

"Flypaper," I said.

"Yeah, I kind of figured that. Can I ask why?"

"It was supposed to be like a frog tongue. Sticky. To catch bugs."

"Huh," he said. "No offense, Finley, but it just looked like a giant orange blob."

"Listen, we're not here to discuss my artwork, okay? Here," I said, thrusting the science notebook at him. "Read fast. I'm not hiding anything; it's the whole *Life Cycle*. But I put sticky notes on stuff about you specifically."

"You expect me to read all this? In five minutes?"

"Okay, so just read the sticky notes, if you want."

"Why exactly would I *want* to?"

"Zachary, listen—I wasn't insulting you; I was *complimenting* you. See?" I flipped through the sticky notes. "There's more," I added. "Those are just the main parts."

He read a little, then looked straight at me. "What about that 'evolving in reverse' stuff? That was kind of an insult, Finley."

"Well, yes. But I was upset at you when I wrote that. You were hanging with the Croakers. Which is fine, you have every right to, but."

Zachary smiled. "They're not so bad."

"I never said they were *bad*. All I ever said—I mean, wrote—was that you were better." There, I'd admitted it. Something I'd never said to any boy, in the history of Finley Davis. "So can we please stop this stupid war?"

"Sure," Zachary said quietly.

"Good." I took a breath. "Because Maya is in trouble. And I think it might help if we went to Fisher-Greenglass together and explained all this amphibian business, but that we've worked it out. I mean maturely, like we're all ready for high school."

"But isn't Maya in trouble with Hairy Hands?"

"Yeah, she is. But we can't help her with that. We *can* help her with the locker business if we all take responsibility, tell the principal we're sorry, swear it won't happen again. I mean, I'm *hoping* we can."

"So am I," Zachary said. In this light you could see

shadows under his eyes, like he hadn't been sleeping very well lately. Although neither was I, so it wasn't too surprising. Anyhow, he'd been back in Fulton long enough to get the sort of winter skin we all had—shadowy, tired-looking, the kind of complexion that looks its worst under school fluorescent lighting.

Which was a shame, really, considering how tan he'd been when he'd arrived from Florida. And that was when? Like two weeks ago? Time had gotten so strange lately, I thought. It was getting hard to keep track.

He handed me back the *Life Cycle*. And maybe it was because his sweatshirt arms were a little short, or they'd shrunk in the wash, or something, but all of a sudden I spotted the ink on his wrist.

"So now can I ask you a question?" I said, as I slipped the binder into my backpack.

"Sure, I guess."

"Your wrist says 'lunch,' doesn't it?"

"No," he said, frowning. "I already told you that once. Remember?"

Of course I remembered. But he'd lied then, out on the snowy field, and we were being honest now. I mean, I'd showed him the complete *Life Cycle*, and practically confessed to him that I had a crush. In the past tense.

"Well, I know it says something *like* 'lunch,' because I saw it," I said. And I don't know what came over me then, but all of a sudden I grabbed his wrist and pulled up the sleeve.

The black letters didn't say *LUNCH*.

They said *CINCH*.

"What does that mean?" I asked. "What's a cinch?"

"Nothing." He was blushing hard.

And I could feel my own cheeks blushing. You know how you can catch yawns from other people? I'm pretty sure you can catch blushes, too.

"Zachary," I said, "I showed you my *Life Cycle*. Now it's your turn to tell the truth, okay? What's a cinch?"

He didn't answer.

"What's a cinch?"

"Girls," he blurted.

"Girls?" I repeated. *"Girls?"*

"That's not what I think," Zach added quickly. "It's what Kieran says, my stepbrother in Florida, remember? And it's just like a memory trick."

"You mean a mnemonic device?"

"Yeah. To help me remember."

"Remember what?" I stared at him. "You have amnesia?"

"No, no. It's just a few tips Kieran gave me about social things. No loud laughing, no dumb jokes about boogers, grow my hair over my ears, stuff like that."

"And he also said stuff about girls?"

"Yeah."

"Like what?"

He looked away. "Finley, forget it, all right?"

"No," I said firmly. "Too late. I'm not forgetting anything."

I peeked at Ms. Krieger. She tapped on her wristwatch and mouthed the words *One more minute*. I nodded back at her, and mouthed the words *I know*.

"All right," Zachary said finally. "Here it is. When I went down to Florida last spring, I felt like a loser. I don't know, like Freakazoid. So Kieran gave me five rules to follow, but I couldn't always remember them, so he turned the first letters into an acronym: *CINCH*."

"So *CINCH* stands for something."

"Yeah. Like HOMES or ROY G BIV."

"Yes, I got that," I said impatiently. "What do the letters stand *for*?"

"It's kind of private. You're sure you really want to—"

"Tell me, Zachary!"

"Whatever, fine." He shrugged. "*C* is for 'contact,' especially eye contact. Kieran said people like it if you look them right in the eye."

"Especially girls?"

"Uh-huh."

Especially if your irises are almost purple. "Keep going," I encouraged.

"*I* is for 'interest.' Kieran said if you want people to like you, show an interest in what they're interested in."

"Like photography?"

"Whatever. It doesn't matter. Ask them questions, compliment them, tell them it's a cool hobby."

"And they'll believe it, right? What's *N*?"

"*N* is 'names.' Kieran says to say people's names when you're talking to them."

"By people you mean girls?"

He nodded. "According to Kieran, girls like it when you use their names in a sentence."

"Do they. How profound."

"He knows a lot of girls, actually. Although he has a girlfriend."

"Lucky her. What's the other *C*?"

"Um."

"You forgot? It's not much of a mnemonic, if you can't even—"

"No, I remember." He started tapping his foot. "The other *C* is for 'chance.' He said to admit I screwed up last year, and to ask for a second chance."

"Which you do, by the way. Constantly." It was funny, but my mouth was feeling dusty. "What's *H*?"

"Okay. So you know how much I grew this past year? I feel kind of weird about it."

"Why?"

"Because it's freakish. I used to be incredibly short, and now suddenly I'm incredibly tall. But I don't *feel* any different; I'm still majorly uncoordinated. And people expect boys to be athletic, especially when they're big, so Kieran said to say I'm working on my hook shot."

"*H* is for 'hook shot'?"

"Yeah," Zachary said.

So that explained why he wouldn't shoot hoops with Maya and me in the gym. "Hook shot" was just a thing to say. It wasn't true; he still couldn't play basketball.

I took a deep, shaky breath. "And the idea is that if you do all this, if you follow Kieran's five easy rules, girls will be a quote-unquote cinch?"

"Well, theoretically. According to Kieran."

"Well, thank you for these valuable insights," I said, standing. "You two have clearly solved the mystery of middle school girls."

"And now you're mad at me?" Zachary asked.

"Uh. Yeah?"

"Why? For CINCH? But it was just a dumb mnemonic!"

"Oh please," I sputtered. "You followed those stupid rules. You believed them. You wrote *CINCH* on your *wrist*, didn't you? And you obviously think all girls are the same, just this giant generic blob."

"No, no." He looked up at me with round, surprised eyes. "The CINCH stuff wasn't about *insulting* anyone. It was just supposed to organize things in my mind. Exactly like the *Life Cycle*."

"You know what?" I snapped. "I'm sorry I even showed you the *Life Cycle*. You don't deserve all the stupid sticky notes."

"Wait. Finley—"

"I'll meet you at the principal's office today after

school. You'd better show up. And don't say my name, either, all right?"

Then I ran out of the library.

I went to the bathroom instead of Spanish.

And I turned on the hand dryer to drown out my thoughts.

CHAPTER 24

"Fin, I really think we should go in there with you," Olivia said. School had just ended, and we were standing in front of the principal's office. "Because we were just as involved as you and Maya."

"Well, not *just*," Hanna reminded her. But she didn't add, *I warned you it was vandalism. And all I did was act as lookout, remember?*

"Thanks," I told them. "But if you guys come in with Zachary and me, it might seem unfair to the boys, like it's all of us girls ganging up. And the whole point is to tell Fisher-Greenglass that we *had* a war going on, but it's totally over now, it's past tense, so she doesn't think Maya might do something else."

"You think it'll work?" Olivia asked, wrinkling her nose. "Because with Hairy Hands involved—"

"Maya can't get in trouble again. So we need to try."

We watched Zachary coming down the hall with Drew and Ben walking closely behind him.

"Hey," Zachary said. His face was pale, and his eyes didn't meet mine, like he thought I was mad at him. Well, if he thought that, he was right. Because I was.

"Let's get this over with," he said quietly.

"Okay, but what are they doing here?" I said, pointing at Drew and Ben.

"We heard Maya might get kicked out of school," Drew said. "So if you need us to say something . . ." He shrugged.

"That's ridiculous," I said scornfully. "No one's getting expelled over a blob of flypaper!"

Although as I said this, it occurred to me I had no idea what people got expelled over. Up until last week, Maya and I had thought Zachary had been expelled for fighting with Jarret. It was funny—if you could use a word like "funny" in these circumstances—how things had changed since Zachary had arrived. Returned.

And of course, if flypapering Señor Hansen's room

didn't get Maya expelled, it would get her yanked from gymnastics. Which was almost as horrible.

"We should go in," Zachary murmured. Still not looking at me.

"Just wait out here, okay?" I said to Drew, Ben, Olivia, and Hanna. "Don't leave, in case she wants to talk to you. Um, and thanks," I added to Drew and Ben.

They nodded seriously.

And then Zachary followed me over to Ms. Hanrahan, the principal's secretary, who for some bizarre reason had decorated her desk with assorted trolls.

She pursed her lips at us, like she had just sucked on a big lemon. "Yes?"

"We'd like to talk to Ms. Fisher-Greenglass," I said. "Please."

"What about?" Mrs. Hanrahan tapped on her mouse with a bubble-gum-colored fingernail.

"Crimes against humanity," Zachary said.

Oh no, was he getting weird now? I jabbed his back with my thumb.

"An incident," I said. "Behavioral."

Mrs. Hanrahan's perfectly tweezed eyebrows rose.

"Involving school property," I added.

She aimed a fingernail at the door. "Go ahead in."

My stomach knotted.

Ms. Fisher-Greenglass was on her cell when we walked into her office, so she pointed to two seats in front of her desk. Her office was surprisingly messy—stacks of papers on the floor, an overfull garbage can, a few overgrown plants tangling up her windowsill. But somehow the mess made me feel a teeny bit calmer. A person who tolerated messes would tolerate youthful hijinks, wouldn't they?

"Let's assume we can reschedule," she said into her phone. "I'll be in touch in the a.m."

On the other hand, I thought, using "a.m." for "morning" sounded too businesslike. Not youthful-hijinks-friendly. Possibly a bad sign, actually.

"Yes?" she said, finally, making her face go neutral, which was probably a skill they taught you in principal school. "And what brings you two here this fine afternoon?"

"Flypaper," I said.

"Ah, yes." She folded her hands.

"Which was actually my fault, not Maya's. But I was just trying to make a sticky frog tongue—"

"To get back at me for the pizza box," Zachary said. "And the croaking and the water."

"Which was obnoxious. But it was all payback for the *Life Cycle*—"

"Which was also obnoxious. Although it was private. Until it wasn't."

"Okay," Ms. Fisher-Greenglass cut in. "Can we please back up here for a minute?"

But Zachary ignored her. He was looking at me, blinking. "What I mean," he said, "is that we both did a bunch of stupid things, okay? But I still think of you as a friend, Finley—not as a generic blob or a dumb mnemonic, but as a person. Because truthfully, who cares what you wrote in that *Life Cycle*? What matters is how you acted. And you never treated me like Freakazoid, even when I was Freakazoid. So if you're in trouble now, or Maya is—"

"Zachary," Ms. Fisher-Greenglass said sternly. "I'm having a hard time following all this. And I thought we were discussing the flypaper."

"We are," Zachary answered. "But just punish me, not Maya or Finley, okay? I'm not even staying at this school, anyhow."

"What?" I gaped at him. My cheeks flushed hot,

and at the same time my hands went cold. It was weird, like my body was in two different time zones. "You're *not*?"

He shook his head. "My dad wants me back in Florida next week, to finish the school year down there. My mom has these, whatever, work commitments. A bunch of travel overseas, I don't know."

"Oh." I swallowed.

"There's this whole custody thing they're working out." Zachary was staring at the principal's tangled plants, which were suddenly lit up by the pale winter sunshine. "I thought they'd agreed on me staying here permanently, but apparently not."

"That isn't right," I managed to say. "To change their minds on you like that."

"Yeah, I guess. But it's important for my mom, so . . ." Now Zachary was staring past the plants, out the window, as if he were already gone from school, already back in Florida with his dad. In a completely different time zone.

And I thought what an idiot I was, how selfish, to be dragging him into the principal's office when he was dealing with all of that at home. But he should have said something in the hallway, before we came in here. Or a few hours ago, in the library, when I shoved the *Life Cycle* at him. And fought with him about that stupid *CINCH* tattoo.

Because how was I supposed to know things if he didn't tell me?

And then telling me *here*, in front of the principal? *Now*, when we'd come to defend Maya?

It just seemed unfair. To all of us. All of it.

Fisher-Greenglass unfolded her hands. "Yes, Zachary, your mom called me with the news this morning. I told her I was really sorry to hear it, because you were doing so well. Especially socially."

He shrugged. I didn't know what else to do, so I nodded.

Fisher-Greenglass added, "And I'm sure many of your classmates will miss you."

She caught my eye and gave me a sympathetic smile, like she understood that Zachary's news affected me, too. The principal was actually a nice person, I thought. But she couldn't fix this.

Nobody talked. The bell rang. We could hear a bunch of kids laughing loudly out in the hallway, and then Ms. Hanrahan call out, "*Walk*, please," followed by more laughing and the sound of frantic running.

Ms. Fisher-Greenglass cleared her throat and said, "So about all this flypaper nonsense: I take it there's been some back-and-forth between the eighth-grade boys and girls?"

"Yes, but it's over now," I said.

"Good to hear that, Finley. You know, you certainly caused Mr. Lundquist some extra work, and we could have had a pest infestation from those crumbs. And I'm not just talking about houseflies. Also, I don't know if the flypaper fumes were toxic, but they were certainly unpleasant."

Irk. Something else I hadn't thought about.

"Sorry," I mumbled. "They were supposedly organic."

"Even if they were, that doesn't mean the whole school should have been inhaling them." She studied my face for a few seconds. "All right, Finley," she finally said. "I haven't decided anything official yet, but I can tell you there'll be a service project in your future involving some sort of payback to the school— maybe assisting Ms. Krieger in the library."

"Oh, sure, fine with me," I said quickly.

"As for Maya, she has a few things to iron out with Señor Hansen, but we're in the process of working on that. I can't tell you very much right now, just that she'll be back in school on Monday, and she'll have some sort of service project as well." Ms. Fisher-Greenglass turned back to Zachary, and suddenly her voice was kind again. "Zachary, the thing for you right now is to get yourself home. It sounds to me like you need to start packing."

"Yeah," he murmured. "I do. Um, well, so thanks for everything."

They both stood. He hesitated for a second; then he threw his arms around her in a Maya-style squeeze.

It was excruciating to watch. But I did.

He bolted out of the office without even glancing in my direction. I sat there for a second, in shock.

In the same sort of sympathetic voice, Ms. Fisher-Greenglass said, "You okay, then, Finley?"

"Me?" I said. "Oh, sure, yes, perfect."

And I zombie-walked out to the lobby area, where everyone was still waiting.

CHAPTER 25

After dinner that night, I offered to help Mom give Max and Addie their baths. The way we did it was Mom and Max in the kitchen, me with Addie in the upstairs bathtub. It was surprisingly fun; I sang "The Eensy-Weensy Spider" while I was shampooing her wispy hair, and Addie loved it so much she kept demanding "AGAIN." The amazing thing was, by the end of the bath she knew most of the words. And I had to admit that, for a two-year-old, my little sister was pretty smart.

As for Max . . . well, when Mom was finished with him, her T-shirt was soaked, but she was beaming.

"It works *so* much better one-on-one," she said. "No more double baths ever again, I swear."

"I'll help you with the baths, if you want," I said. "I don't mind."

Mom gave me a wet hug. "Thank you, Awesome Daughter," she said into my hair.

After the Terrible Two were finally in their toddler beds, I closed my bedroom door. Mom and Dad were going to take my camera for a month, but starting tomorrow, so tonight I decided to take my own photo. A selfie, I guess you could call it. I wasn't even thinking about the yearbook—it was too late to submit photos, anyway. But I still wanted some picture of myself that wasn't generic. That wasn't just *Eighth-Grade Girl Smiling for the Camera.* That showed *me*, or at least how I felt right then. Even if what I felt was a muddled, tangled mess.

Because what if I wanted to remember it someday? This photo might be what I had instead of a memory.

I stood in front of my mirror for a long time, like fifteen minutes. But all I saw was a pool-noodle-shaped girl with too many freckles and boring brown hair.

What other people saw. Nothing hidden behind my eyes or underneath my skin. No secrets, no mystery, no weirdness.

I picked up my camera. Maybe if I zoomed in on myself I'd notice something shocking. Or if I used the wide angle I could get some sort of ugly/beautiful distortion.

I pressed the buttons. Then I looked in the mirror, watching myself press the buttons.

What I saw was myself, with a camera covering my face.

Click.

There it was. My self-portrait.

A couple of weeks later, I asked Ms. Fisher-Greenglass for Zachary's e-mail address. For some reason I couldn't explain, I'd decided to e-mail him my self-portrait. And as long as I was attaching photos, I sent him the four photos I'd taken on the stairwell after he'd (accidentally) noticed the *Life Cycle* and I'd (mistakenly) invited him to Chloe's party.

To go with the photos I wrote this note:

Hey Zachary,
I thought you might like to see these. I still don't know what I'm doing, but I guess I'm learning. Ish.
I'm sorry we ended on a fight. I still think your step-

brother's mnemonic was dumb and that his view of girls was totally lame. But maybe the Life Cycle *wasn't that different, so probably we're even in messing up. Anyhow, I hope we can be friends in the future.*

I liked that last sentence. It didn't say, *Everything is fine between us, lalala,* because honestly, I didn't know if that was true.

But I did hope we could be friends sometime. So that part wasn't a lie.

The ending of the note was tricky. I didn't want to end it with "love," because I didn't. "Talk to you soon" was out because I didn't know if we would. "Best" was too formal, "ciao" was too pretentious, and "sincerely" was too . . . I don't know. Unsmiling.

So in the end I decided on "See you, Finley."

Because the funny thing was, when I looked at the stairwell photos, I realized I had.

A few days later, Zachary e-mailed back:

Hey Finley,
Thanks for the photos. They're great, although I have to say I look a little slimy. And green. But maybe I was

feeling sort of amphibian that day? It's possible.

It's okay here, and school is mostly pretty decent, considering it's school. I'm not sorry I came back to Fulton, but it was probably not the best idea to show up in the middle of the year, even with so-called "tips" from Kieran. Some things you have to figure out as you go along, I guess.

Anyhow, right now my plan is to come back to Fulton in the fall and start high school with everyone else. Restart, whatever. It will NOT be a CINCH. But my mom got another promotion, which means she won't be traveling all the time now, so both my parents say they're willing to give it a shot.

Not a hook shot, so don't worry.

Really sorry if I hurt your feelings, Finley. The truth is I've always thought of you in 3-D. So maybe next time send a hologram of yourself instead of a photo? Haha, joke.

See you in a few months. I'm usually pretty lazy over the summer, but if you e-mail or text, promise I'll answer.

—Zach

Zach, I thought. He'd changed his identity again. But it sounded right—I couldn't say why, but he seemed like a Zach.

Zach. Zach Mattison.

For some reason, I was smiling.

CHAPTER 26

Anyway, that's everything that happened in the past tense.

Now it's ten-thirty p.m. on September 2, the night before the First Day of High School. My clothes are all picked out, my backpack is empty, my phone is charged, my nails are polished, and my stomach feels like a tangled blob of flypaper. I'm hoping I won't get lost as I look for my classrooms; I'm hoping my teachers are as nice as Ms. Krieger and Ms. Fisher-Greenglass and not as evil as Hairy Hands. I'm hoping I see Maya at lunch, and Olivia and Hanna, too, that I make the basketball team, that I get to take photos for the newspaper.

Also: I'm hoping Zachary—I mean Zach—meets me in the library, the way we planned.

I want to see him from the beginning.

MEET BRITTANY, CASSIE, AND ISABEL.

THREE GIRLS WITH BIG DREAMS AND BIG AMBITIONS.

Sometimes the drama during the commercials is better than what happens during the show. And sometimes the drama making the commercial is even better. . . .